A dream date . . . with the wrong girl.

I stepped off the ice rink and made my way to the snack bar. By the time I ordered two hot chocolates, fifteen minutes had gone by. Miranda still hadn't shown up.

But when my order appeared, a laugh rang through the snack bar. A familiar bell-toned laugh. Caroline!

I grabbed the two hot chocolates and headed out to the booths. Caroline was there, her back to me, laughing nonstop. Sitting across from her, gesturing wildly, was Wade Hamilton.

My last attempt to set her up worked after all, I thought, feeling a little relieved.

But as the minutes passed, I could feel my face burning a little. Caroline and I always had fun when we were hanging out together, but I had never seen her laugh as hard as she was laughing now.

On dates with Miranda, I sometimes felt like I was holding back a little, like I was afraid to be myself. Caroline didn't seem to be having that problem with Wade. How could she let him get so close to her so soon?

Caroline was having the time of her life while I was sitting alone in the snack bar with two cups of cold hot chocolate.

This wasn't how I had imagined my perfect date.

Don't miss any of the books in *Love Stories*
—the romantic series from Bantam Books!

KISSING
Caroline

Cheryl Zach

BANTAM BOOKS
NEW YORK · TORONTO · LONDON · SYDNEY · AUCKLAND

RL 6, age 12 and up

KISSING CAROLINE

A Bantam Book / December 1996

Produced by Daniel Weiss Associates, Inc.
33 West 17th Street
New York, NY 10011.

ISBN: 0-553-57014-5

Published simultaneously in the United States and Canada

Bantam Books are published by Bantam Books, a division of Bantam
Doubleday Dell Publishing Group, Inc. Its trademark, consisting of the
words "Bantam Books" and the portrayal of a rooster, is Registered in
U.S. Patent and Trademark Office and in other countries. Marca
Registrada. Bantam Books, 1540 Broadway, New York, New York 10036.

PRINTED IN THE UNITED STATES OF AMERICA

OPM   0 9 8 7 6 5 4 3

This book is dedicated, with love, to my future son-in-law, Brad Place, and all his great Michigan family, especially Claudia, Glenn, Brian, Kelly, and Jerry.

ONE

SHE GLIDED OVER the snow like an angel without wings. Her long, cornsilk hair poured over her shoulders; her delicate feet barely left prints in the glittering white powder beneath her. I waited, breathless.

"Miranda," I called, reaching out to her, waiting for the moment when she came close enough for me to take her in my arms and kiss her like I had done on so many other nights.

But as she approached, her beautiful face grew concerned. "What's wrong?" I asked, wondering what horrible thing could possibly make Miranda look so sad.

"I'm sorry, Jake," she said, each word escaping her mouth with a misty, clouded breath. "But I think it's time that you and I both—"

Bam! Bam! Bam!

1

"Wake *up, Jake,*" my little sister, Kristen, pleaded from outside my bedroom door, her voice slightly muffled. "You *promised* you'd help me put up the garland." She pounded on my door again, more persistently this time.

Sprawled across the bed, I tried to ignore her. Not that I had actually been sleeping or anything. How could any guy sleep after having his heart broken? Not just broken, but *stomped* on! I wasn't sure which would be worse: to keep lying around having nightmares about the night Miranda broke up with me or to help my little sister hang up Christmas decorations.

"Please, Jake," Kristen pleaded. "You know I can't reach it."

According to my clock, it was 11:37. I'd been sleeping in later and later on Saturdays after Miranda broke up with me. I just didn't feel like getting out of bed. But Kristen *was* trying to be nice, as much as little sisters can be. Kristen was only twelve, and I was sixteen and a half, the big brother. She needed my help, and I needed something to do. Pushing myself up from the rumpled bed, I walked over and unlocked the door.

When it swung open, Kristen stared at me. "Boy, you look awful," she said, eyeing my faded old U2 T-shirt and flannel boxers I'd been sleeping in for the past week. "Just because that dumb girl dumped you, you don't have to fall apart."

That was *not* the right thing to say. Giving Kristen my chilliest *go-away* stare, I started to shut the door.

"No, wait, I'm sorry," she said quickly, stepping over the threshold to block the door. "Please, Jake?"

"No more comments about my love life," I told her, frowning. "You don't know anything about it." I ran my fingers through my hair. It felt even more unruly than usual.

"Your life or love in general? I just read in a column in *Teen* about how to tell if a boy really loves you—or if a girl loves you, in your case, and—"

I leaned against the door. "I don't have the time *or* the patience, Kristen."

She held up both hands. "Sorry, sorry. I'll shut up, I promise. The stuff's in the hall."

Fifteen minutes later I was outside. The chill of a Michigan winter morning was a sharp contrast to the warm quilt I'd been buried under a short while ago. I picked up the big carton of artificial garland that sat next to the stepladder on the front stoop, waiting for me. *Let me get this over with,* I resolved to myself as I set up the ladder. Picking up an armload of prickly plastic garland, I climbed the steps, barely avoiding an icy patch.

"Be careful," urged Kristen.

I grunted. Falling and breaking my neck would be a definite downer.

3

The garland didn't take long to arrange—I helped put it up every Christmas—and when I finished, I stepped down and jumped off the stoop to admire my handiwork, rubbing a sore thumb where the garland had pricked me.

Kristen adjusted the red bows at the side. "It looks great, Jake. Mom will be so happy we got it up already." I didn't have to ask—I knew my mom was out running errands. Every Saturday from eight to two she was driving all around Grand Rapids—the library, the grocery store, the dry cleaners—she was a Saturday dynamo.

"Dad promised that we'll get our tree next weekend," Kristen said, skidding on a pool of ice.

Nodding, I folded the ladder and picked up the hammer and box of nails. I knew I was acting zombified, but I couldn't stop myself. When was I going to be myself again? *When Miranda comes back,* I answered silently. *When she realizes that we were meant to be together.*

"Put the garland box back in the attic," I told Kristen, my tone flat. "I'll take this stuff to the garage."

My arms full, I turned, almost colliding with my best friend, Sid Halleman. He stepped back quickly, a plastic-wrapped plate in his gloved hand.

"Whoa," he said, balancing the plate. "You almost turned these into crumbs." He took a closer

4

look at my face and shook his head. "You got bags the size of steamer trunks under your eyes. Didn't you sleep at all last night?"

Kristen muttered, "Dumb girl."

"Don't get her started, Halleman," I warned, trying to smile in spite of the pain I was feeling. I knew my little sister was trying to be sympathetic, but all she was doing was rubbing it in. As if she knew anything about love anyway.

Luckily Sid got the hint and lifted the plate to distract her.

Kristen took the bait. "What have you got?"

"My mother sent you guys some Hanukkah cookies," Sid explained. "She's testing a new recipe for my kid brother's holiday party at school."

"Yummy," Kristen said. "I *love* your mother's cookies." Taking the plate from Sid, she went into the house, sniffing the cookies happily.

Sid followed me to the garage. "Nice save, huh?" he pointed out. Sid lives next door, and I could count on him dropping by at least twice a day.

"Yeah, right. I know I look bad, Sid, but watch what you say in front of Kristen next time, okay?" I tossed the tools back where they belonged for emphasis. "How'd you like to have your little brother telling you how to handle your life?"

Sid leaned against a folded lawn chair. "Sorry. It's just hard to figure out why Miranda would do something like that, you know? I guess I still can't believe you two broke up."

"You mean, why *she* broke up with *me*." I slammed the stepladder onto its hook in the garage wall. "This wasn't just *any* girl, Sid. This is *Miranda* we're talking about. She was perfect—the girl I'd dreamed of meeting my whole life. And she was *mine*. Don't you understand?"

Sid nodded, but I wasn't sure he meant it. Sid was a casual-date kind of guy. He had never been in love—never had his heart broken. Not like me.

I wondered who would really understand. Not Sid—he doesn't know the first thing about serious relationships. I wished I knew someone who could relate.

"Paging Jake Magee," Sid joked, waving to get my attention. "Mr. Magee, would you please pick up the white courtesy phone?"

"Sorry, Sid," I apologized. "I've just got a lot on my mind."

"I know, man. I'm real sorry about you and Miranda. That's gotta hurt."

Don't I know it, I thought, looking at my best friend squarely. "Remember when we were in eighth grade, Sid? We used to talk about girls—"

"A lot," Sid agreed, a devilish grin creeping across his face. "Not to mention studying those *Playboy*s I stole from my cousin, remember?" He rolled his eyes.

I ignored him. "You always wanted to fall for a redhead with big brown eyes and a nice body. She should like all kinds of sports and not giggle."

Sid nodded.

"And my perfect girl would be blond, with long hair and blue eyes. She would love animals and enjoy outdoors stuff, like camping."

"Does Miranda like to camp?" Sid asked.

"I guess I'll never find out," I admitted, sighing. "We were planning to do something in the spring, but that's not going to happen now."

Miranda was my first real girlfriend. Most girls I met didn't compare with the picture I had in my mind—that's why Miranda hit me like a thunderbolt. She was a home run from the moment I saw her; a sweet three pointer. Right away I knew she was perfect.

I'd already asked her to the Winter Formal, and I'd been saving all my money from my part-time job at Hillcrest Kennels to buy her a really special Christmas present. And now—after one single sentence from Miranda's lips—everything was off. My heart was in pieces, just like I'd heard in one of those corny, old-fashioned love songs. Life was rotten. Rotten and unfair. Rotten and unfair and . . .

"Hey, snap out of it." Sid punched me lightly on the arm. "What do you say we eat some cookies?"

"I'm not hungry."

7

Sid shook his head. "You *are* in bad shape. Okay, let's go hang out at the mall."

"I don't—"

"Jake! Get a grip." He held his arms out stiffly in front of him and made a zombie face. I took a swing at him—not hard, but he stepped out of reach anyhow. "You're losing it, Magee. You need to get out of your house. You need to get back on your feet."

He was right, I realized sadly. My life was in shreds. If I didn't start dealing with it, it'd deal with me instead.

"Oh, okay. The mall it is." The way I felt, it didn't much matter where I went.

I walked in the house to get some cash and my gloves and found Kristen at the kitchen table, a glass of milk and the already depleted plate of cookies in front of her.

"I'm heading to the mall," I said.

She gulped down milk excitedly. "Ooh, take me," she begged.

"No way. Tell Mom I'll be back by five."

"I'll think about it," she retorted, sticking out a crumb-covered tongue. "Besides, I wouldn't want to go with you anyway. You're no fun these days, Jake."

It was the last Saturday in November, and everyone from our side of Grand Rapids, Michigan, seemed to be at the mall. The decora-

8

tions here made our little garland at home look pretty insignificant. Everywhere I turned, red velvet bows garnished store windows, and giant red-and-white candy canes dangled from the ceiling.

Everything was so festive and cheerful. I sighed. Without Miranda, I had no reason to celebrate this year.

"Just watching you drags me down, Magee," Sid complained. "Can't you *pretend* to be happy, at least?"

"Wish I could," I told him.

Sid shook his head. "You go mope, then. I've got to check out what's new at the bookstore. Meet you there in twenty, okay?"

He dashed off, leaving me to sit by myself on a bench at the side of the mall. *Why was Sid so quick to bolt on me?* I wondered. *Am I that much of a drag? I'd better get my act together before my best friend dumps me too.* I was staring at a melting ice-cream cone in a nearby trash can when raised voices made me look up.

A tall gangly guy and a girl with long brown hair were arguing fiercely—none of my business. But as I turned away I noticed a pool of liquid was spreading on the floor. The girl held an empty paper cup in one hand, and there was a big stain on her light blue leggings. The guy was holding the girl's elbows. I watched as he shook her, hard.

9

What kind of jerk would push a girl around like that? I wondered, my face blazing with the realization that this idiot had a girlfriend and I didn't. Where was the justice in that? *He doesn't deserve a girlfriend if he doesn't know how to treat her.*

Before I realized what I was doing, I stood up and started walking toward the couple, my sneakers squeaking against the tile floor. The noise made the guy glance over at me briefly, but he turned back to the girl and growled under his breath, his hand still tight on her arm.

"Hey, who do you think you are?" I blurted. It wasn't until he turned and threw me a blazingly angry look that I realized he was Brian White, star of the Hillcrest High School basketball team.

"Stay out of this," Brian barked, not even looking at me. "This is between me and her."

I tried to ignore him, but it's not easy to ignore Brian White. Turning to the girl, I asked, "Is he hurting you?"

She shook her head. "No, it's just—"

He reached across and shoved me. "Hey, when I tell you to get lost, you don't ask any more questions."

Right then I knew that I'd had enough. I don't know if it was my frustration over losing Miranda or my getting tired of all the nagging questions from my friends and family, but one thing was for sure: I'd gone through too much to put up with a Neanderthal suffering from a superiority complex. So I did something I never would have imagined doing before—I shoved him back.

I shoved Brian White, superjock.

It felt like something I had been needing to do for days. It was a release.

It felt *good*.

But instead of making what I thought would be an inevitable retaliation, Brian just backed off. "That's it. I'm out of here," he snapped, raising his hands in front of him. "I'm not playing any more of your reindeer games, Caroline. Why don't you and Rudolph make a break for the North Pole before I change my mind?" Turning on his heel, he stomped away.

"Brian! Come back!" the girl cried, looking as if she was about to break down. "Brian, don't be like that, please!"

I just didn't get it. Here I'd just prevented this poor girl from getting her arm torn off and she was asking for this loser to come *back?*

"Excuse me," I began tentatively, "but if you don't mind my asking—aren't you better off *without* a guy like that? I thought he was going to rip you in half there for a second."

She turned to me; the angry look in her eyes took me totally by surprise. "Why don't you mind your own business?" she asked, dabbing at her leggings with a tissue.

11

"I thought he was—I mean—your drink is spilled all over you, and he was shoving—"

"He wasn't shoving me! We were just talking. A little kid ran into me and knocked my drink out of my hands." She frowned at me. "You'd better get your eyes checked before you *really* get yourself in trouble."

The whole thing still made no sense. I didn't want to belabor the point, but the sarcasm in her voice made me want to keep going. "But he was arguing with you, wasn't he?"

She sighed and clammed up a little. "That was—that was none of your business."

"But if he was trying to hurt you—"

"He was trying to hurt me, but not how you think." She crumpled her empty cup furiously. "He was breaking up with me, okay? Are you satisfied now, Sherlock?" A tear ran down her cheek. "I was trying to talk him out of it, but I think *you* handled everything from that point on."

Way to go, Magee. I could just see the headlines now: MISERABLE GIRL PUSHES NOSY DO-GOODER DOWN ESCALATOR IN MALL DISTURBANCE. "Sorry," was all I could say.

She sniffed and brushed the tear away, just as another one fell. "What's the difference anyway. Like it even matters."

I noticed a few shoppers staring at us. I realized that they probably thought *I* was the guy who was making her upset. "Uh, you seem okay, I guess," I

12

said, fumbling for a way out. "I'm sorry I butted into your business. I really am."

She relented just a bit. "You were only trying to help, right?"

"Right," I said. "Sorry again." I walked away, but the image of her tear-stained face stayed in my mind.

TWO

SANTA CLAUS—OR ONE of his many "helpers," as my folks had me believing when I was young—sat on a big throne in the center courtyard of the mall, holding a squirming kid on his lap.

Just last week Miranda and I stood hand in hand, watching a similar scene. We had joked about getting our pictures taken on Santa's lap and guessed what each of the kids might have been asking for.

"A Surfside Susie with her Pastel Pony," she had guessed for a shy girl in a frilly dress. "And that kid wants a Mashed-Potato Monster Maker." She'd pointed out a boy with a wild cowlick.

"No, he's more the Tai Chi Tommy type. With action grip, of course," I'd offered, and she'd giggled and held my hand tighter.

"You're so silly, Jake," she had said, standing on her toes to rub my nose with hers.

I had leaned down, brushed my cheek against her silky hair, and kissed her forehead tenderly. "I love to make you laugh . . ." I kissed her cheek. "To make you smile . . ." I kissed her lips. Again and again . . .

"And I love you, Jake," she had whispered, cupping my face in her hands and kissing me back as Christmas carolers sang in the background. "We love each other. That's everything to me."

Today a long line stretched around the gigantic Christmas tree in the mall courtyard, just like it had then. Dozens of little kids waited with their moms and dads to tell Santa what they wanted for Christmas.

I knew what I wanted. But I couldn't have it.

Sid punched my arm. "Stop it," he said. "You're zoning out again, I can tell."

"Okay, okay." This trip to the mall was only making me feel worse. Not only couldn't I get Miranda out of my mind, but I was still bothered by that weird scene with Brian White and his girlfriend.

"Look, Magee, I've still got to buy some Hanukkah presents. Do you want to join me or take off?"

"Well . . . I'll just look around by myself, I guess."

"Okay. Meet you at the car at four-thirty?"

"Gotcha," I replied, turning away. At the edge of the center court I noticed a smaller tree decorated only with small paper cutouts.

Walking closer, I saw that each cutout was a paper angel, and there were names on each one. A big poster read, Adopt an Angel for Christmas!

A table had been set up at the side of the tree. A middle-aged lady sat at one end, with a clipboard in front of her, and a girl about my age sat at the other. I stopped. It was the girl from the argument—Brian White's now ex-girlfriend, thanks to me. I started slinking away, but it was no use.

"Can I help—?" a familiar voice piped up. "Oh, no, it's *you* again. Are you going to make me lose my volunteer job too?"

I smiled, embarrassed. "I, uh, I was just wondering . . . what is this anyway?"

"It's for charity," the girl said, her voice tight. "Something you've already tried dishing out today."

She was really making me feel like a jerk. "Listen, Carolyn—"

"Ca-ro-*line*," she corrected me.

"Ca-ro-*line*," I repeated. "I really am interested. What's it for?"

Caroline rolled her eyes, then relented. "The names on our angel tree have been selected by a social service agency. They're disadvantaged children who may not receive any gifts for Christmas.

17

Anyone who would like to help a child can choose a name and buy gifts, which will be delivered to their 'angel' anonymously." She paused. "Any questions?"

"No, thanks," I muttered, turning toward the tree. The project was a good one, I had to admit. I couldn't imagine some little kid who still believed in Santa Claus, believed in the Christmas magic, waking up on Christmas Day and finding no gifts under the tree. Heck, maybe no tree! Trees cost money too.

I stepped closer to the tree and checked out the angel cutouts. There were boys and girls of all different ages. One paper angel caught my eye—Kevin, Age 6. Jeez, six years old and no Christmas.

I'd already taken care of all my Christmas presents for this year. I'd made an oak business card holder for my dad in woodshop, and I had two poinsettias on hold at the local nursery for my mom. And for Kristen I'd bought two new CDs that she'd asked for.

For Miranda, I'd been saving up for a gold silhouette heart pendant with a tiny diamond in it that I'd seen in the jewelry department of the mall's biggest store. I'd almost had enough money saved. But now I didn't have any use for the money I'd worked so hard to earn.

Suddenly I knew what I would do—spend some of that money on Kevin. I'd give someone a reason to celebrate Christmas instead of just moping around and making myself—and everybody else—miserable.

And I couldn't deny taking a certain satisfaction in showing Caroline that I *did* know a thing or two about helping people.

As I took Kevin's angel off the tree another paper cutout caught my eye. Wanted—One Nice Guy to Heal a Broken Heart. There was no name at the top, nothing else to identify who made this request. But I had an idea whose request it was. *And it's partially my fault,* I thought. *Maybe all my fault, come to think of it.* I reached for the anonymous angel, lifted it off the tree, and slipped it into my shirt pocket. Then I walked back to the volunteer table with Kevin's angel in my hand.

When I approached the table, Caroline automatically asked, "Can I help you?" But when she looked up and noticed who I was, her tone became exasperated. "Let me guess. *You* would like to adopt an angel."

"Sure," I said. "I found the one I want." I showed her the angel with Kevin's name on it.

"You're serious about this, aren't you?" she asked, one eyebrow cocked.

"Sure am," I replied. "Isn't a guy allowed to do a good deed when he wants to?"

"Nothing wrong with that," she replied, pulling out a form. "It's just that you hardly fit the description of our average sponsor." She smiled tightly. "Just fill out this form. Bring your gifts to this table by the Friday before Christmas so that we can get them to the children in time for the holidays." It was obviously a reminder she'd given out many times.

After carefully filling out the form, I pushed it back across the table. She glanced over it quickly. "Thanks, uh, Jake. You'll make a little kid very happy. If you actually mean to follow through on this, of course."

"Oh, I mean it," I replied. "In fact—" I pulled out the other angel from my shirt pocket.

"You picked out another angel?" she asked incredulously.

"Not exactly. I just—I just wondered what this was all about?" I showed her the not-so-mysterious message and watched with fascination as a wave of bright red washed over her face and neck.

"That's none of your—uh, this was just—what I meant was . . . um, it's not mine," she muttered, crumpling the angel into a ball and pushing it hastily under a pile of papers.

"Look, you don't have to explain—" I started.

"It's just a prank," she interrupted. Her shoulders dropped heavily. "No, who am I kidding? You know *exactly* what that's all about—"

"I know." I stopped her before she could let loose. "Listen, I feel like it's all my fault. If I hadn't interrupted you guys, you and Brian might have ironed things out. I'm really sorry. I know what it's like to have something like that happen just before the holidays."

"Thank you, Mr. Sensitive," Caroline said. She doodled a candy cane on the notepad in front of her.

"Hey, I mean it," I told her. "I'm going through the same thing right now."

"Really?" She cocked her head to one side. "So you don't normally act this irrational?"

"What do you mean?" I asked, wondering if she was going to go off on me again.

"In the last hour you tried to start a fight with my boyfriend *and* you signed up to buy gifts for charity," Caroline said. "And that's only what *I've* seen."

I laughed a little, and she did too. It felt good to laugh again—I couldn't remember the last time I had.

"Look, I'm really sorry if I messed things up for you," I apologized.

"Hey, these things happen. What can I say?" she responded, but the look of sadness on her face showed she didn't really mean it.

"Could I buy you a Coke or something? I feel like I owe you after what I did today," I finished.

"No, thanks. I—" Caroline paused for a second. "Well, why not," she said, more to herself than me. "We can share stories of how we earned our battle scars."

"Half hour okay?" I asked.

"See you then," she told me.

21

THREE

"THANKS FOR OFFERING to hear me out, Jake," Caroline said as we walked to the food court. "I'm still pretty confused about what happened before." She shrugged. "I should probably ask *you* what happened. I was too stunned to be paying any attention."

"I know exactly how you feel," I replied. "Ever since Miranda—my ex-girlfriend—broke up with me, all I can do is replay the same five minutes in my head over and over and over again, just in case I missed something the first time around."

She shook her head. "What bad timing we have, huh?"

"I know," I replied. "No worse time to be alone than Christmastime. Especially when you were counting on *not* being alone."

We had reached the food court, and Caroline

led me over to the juice bar. "I'll have a lemonade," she told the girl behind the counter as she reached down for the purse that hung at her hip.

I put out my hand. "No, no, it was my idea, and it's my treat." I stood in line and bought two fresh-squeezed lemonades. When I walked away from the counter, we got lucky—another couple was leaving, so I scooted across and grabbed the vacant booth before anyone else could take it.

Laughing, Caroline slipped into the opposite side of the booth. She took a long sip of the lemonade.

"Mmmm, this is good. Thanks, Jake," she told me, fiddling with the straw.

"No problem. It's the least I could do."

Caroline didn't meet my eyes; instead, she stabbed the straw back into her cup. "You know, I have to be honest. I was almost hoping you wouldn't come back."

"Why is that?"

"Well, half of me really needed to talk to some-body, but the other half just wanted to go home and sulk. Either that or find out that Brian called to make up with me." She looked down at the sticky tabletop. "Which I seriously doubt."

"Hey, don't think about that right now," I said, shaking the ice around in my cup. "You've got to do whatever is best for you. I mean, something like this"—I gestured around us—"is a good idea, I think."

"Really?"

"Yeah," I continued. "It's helping me out anyway. I was thinking that I was the only person in the world who got dumped just in time for the holidays."

"Thanks for reminding me," Caroline said, slumping down in her chair a bit. Her long, wavy brown hair fell in her face.

"Sorry, Caroline—I didn't mean it that way. What I meant was, it helps to talk about it. Especially when you meet someone who's in the same boat you are."

Caroline pushed back her hair and looked up at me. "You're right, Jake," she said. "It's just that— it's just that things are a little too fresh for me right now." Her expression grew pained, as if it was all just starting to hit her. But then she straightened up a little and put on a brave smile. "Tell you what. Why don't *you* tell me *your* horror story. Give me all the gory details. In fact, make it extra depressing. Then I'll feel better by comparison."

"Hmmm, that's a tough order," I said. "Because there really *aren't* many gory details. I picked her up for a date, and she flat out told me that she thought it was time we started seeing other people. We had been together for three months." I paused, remembering the perfect, peaceful moment just before she broke the news to me. "The worst part was that it came out of nowhere. I thought everything was going great."

Her smile turned sympathetic. "Well, this fight with Brian hardly came out of nowhere. We've argued before, but we've always been able to work through it. But this is the first time he ever walked away from me and didn't come back." She sighed. "Oh, jeez. I think it really *is* over this time, Jake. But it's not sinking in yet, you know?"

"Well, I hate to scare you," I started, "but when you get home, it'll hit you—hard. If you have pictures up of the two of you or any tokens from past dates—any small thing that could remind you of him in the slightest way is dangerous."

"Great," she said.

"My suggestion is to get a giant vacuum cleaner and suck up everything in your entire room immediately," I said, only half joking. "That way you don't have to look at it. You don't even have to set foot in there."

As I watched Caroline sip the rest of her lemonade I realized how good it felt to get all of this pent-up emotion out of my system. Up until now everyone seemed to treat me as either a basket case going over Niagara Falls or as a scientific specimen that needed to be carefully watched and monitored. Even Sid was no help. All he did was shrug and tell me to quit moping. Well, now I *had* quit moping—and Sid was nowhere in sight.

"I wonder what your girlfriend was thinking, Jake," Caroline began, a sadly mischievous smile creeping across her face. "I mean, aside from the fact that you're nosy, impulsive, overly persistent . . ."

"Hey," I said, giving her a mock warning look. "Brokenhearted guys don't always act like they should. Remember that."

"I'm just kidding." She paused. "But seriously, Jake. You don't seem like such a bad guy. I'm sure you must have treated—what was her name again?"

"Miranda," I replied, the weight of her name making me sink farther down into the booth.

"Miranda Thomas?" she asked. "Blond hair, that Miranda?"

"Yeah." I sat up. "Do you know her?"

"Well, I have a class with her. Do you go to Hillcrest too?"

"Uh-huh," I admitted, surprised. I just assumed that a jock like Brian White would be dating girls from different schools. "I've never seen you around, though."

"I just moved here from Ohio this summer," she replied. "Hillcrest is a pretty big school, a lot bigger than the one I transferred from. I'm still not quite used to it." She looked thoughtful. "Wait a minute. Jake Magee, right?"

"That's me."

"I thought your name was familiar. You write that great sports column in the school paper." She smiled. "Wow, you're practically a celebrity. I read your column every week."

"Not as much of a celebrity as Brian White."

"I guess you would know," she said, huffing a little. "I don't get it, Jake. If you knew who Brian White was, then why did you practically try to start a fight with him?"

"I thought he was going to hurt you, Caroline. Really. I wasn't thinking. I just acted."

She took the top off her lemonade cup and started poking the ice with her straw. Her eyes were downcast. "I guess I should thank you, Jake. All things considered, I was pretty ungrateful. You were only trying to help."

"But I—"

"No buts," she demanded. "Don't take the blame for this. You saw what happened. This is my deal—mine and Brian's. Who knows, maybe he's tried to call and apologize. That's the usual pattern, you know: argue, apologize, argue . . ."

"It's funny you should say that," I said after she trailed off. "I never really had any arguments with Miranda. Everything was going really smoothly. I just don't understand."

"How weird." Caroline's eyes followed a couple who walked by our table, holding hands. Her expression seemed to darken. "That's what I was trying to say before, Jake. You seem like a pretty decent guy. I guess Miranda needs her head examined."

I don't know about that, I thought. *The only thing I'd change about her is the fact that she dumped me.*

"What lunch period do you have, Jake?" Caroline changed the subject abruptly, her voice sounding falsely bright.

"Second shift," I replied absently.

"Hey, me too," she said. "Maybe we could eat lunch together sometime." Caroline went back to stirring her ice while I stared past her shoulder.

Suddenly Caroline slapped her palms down on the table, snapping me to attention. "Hey, we're getting a little gloomy here. Maybe we should call it a day. What do you say?"

It was just then that I noticed that my stomach was growling. I looked at my watch: 4:35. I was supposed to meet Sid five minutes ago.

"Hey, it was great meeting you," I said, jumping up from the table. "But I gotta run."

Caroline nodded. "Me too." She tossed her cup into the trash can—two points. "You know, I'm glad we did this. I feel a little better."

"Not much . . ."

"I know, but some. Now I'll go home and get that big vacuum cleaner ready."

I laughed a little, admiring her courage. "Who knows. Maybe you'll have a message from Brian waiting for you."

Caroline rolled her eyes. "I'd like to think so. But I have a feeling . . ." Her eyes glazed over, and she took a step back with a helpless shrug. "Good night, Jake. I'm glad we met. Friends?" she asked, holding out a hand.

"Friends," I replied, shaking it. "Take care, Caroline."

"You too."

I began making my way down the crowded mall corridor, dodging overfilled shopping bags and cranky kids. Then suddenly I realized that I didn't know Caroline's last name.

"Wait, Caroline!" I called, running back in her direction. "What's your last name?"

She whirled around and brushed her fingers across her cheeks, but not quickly enough. Her face was streaked with tears. "Willis," she said, her voice breaking. "See you at school, Jake," she called before she turned around and began rushing for the nearest door.

It was probably just beginning to sink in for her. I shook my head as I headed for the opposite side of the mall, where Sid was parked. Caroline was really patient, listening to me go on and on about Miranda. I felt better, but she was obviously miserable. Maybe a man-to-man with Brian White would help. If I could get him to apologize to Caroline, maybe she'd feel a little better. Who knows, maybe I'd even help patch things up between them.

I started jogging, knowing Sid was going to be ticked at me for being late.

"Thought you'd run away with the circus," Sid quipped when I met him at the car.

"Very funny." I slid into the passenger seat, and Sid turned the key in the ignition. "You won't believe this, but I walked in on someone's breakup—Brian White's."

"*That* prima donna?" Sid asked. Sid was on the varsity basketball team with Brian, and I knew he had more than his share of opinions about the team's star player—all of them bad. "You've gotta be joking."

"No, I'm serious. And his girlfriend, well, ex-girlfriend, I guess, is really nice. Her name's Caroline Willis. Heard of her?"

"Never."

"Well, we all know Brian doesn't talk much about anyone but himself," I offered.

Sid laughed derisively. "You got that right." Sid popped a Pearl Jam cassette in the tape deck. "So what happened?"

I told him the whole story, from interrupting Brian and Caroline's fight to having a lemonade with her in the food court.

"You shoved Brian White?" Sid let out a low whistle. "Jeez, you do have a death wish."

"He didn't even seem to care, though," I insisted. "He just walked off. I don't know what Caroline was doing with him, to be honest. She seems like a smart girl."

"Is she hot?" Sid asked, wiggling his eyebrows.

Sid was so predictable. "I don't know." I groaned. "Brown hair, hazel eyes. Dresses okay. I didn't really notice."

"Yeah, right." Sid gave me one of his on-the-prowl looks.

"Cut it out, Sid. It's nothing like that," I snapped. "Like I'd even want to *look* at another girl after Miranda."

"Sounds to me like you just did," Sid offered.

I glared at him. "Come on, this is different—"

"*Right.*"

I ignored him for the rest of the ride.

FOUR

"MIRANDA'S AT THE third table," Sid told me under his breath.

"Thanks for telling me," I said as we took our trays to an empty table in the back of the cafeteria. "I'd rather not know."

"I always want to keep you up on the latest," Sid said, digging into his cheeseburger before we even sat down.

Don't look, Magee, I told myself. *You'll only make it worse.* But I had to. There she was—talking to her friend Kara. Miranda looked amazing. Her long blond hair fell sleekly over one shoulder, and her pink sweater made her cheeks glow. *Why does she look even more beautiful to me now than she ever did before?* I wondered. *I didn't think that was possible.*

As I watched, a tall boy leaned across the table

and said something to her. Miranda laughed, and I could see the dimple in her left cheek deepen. *I used to rub my thumb over her dimple, just to see her smile. She always smiled when I did that.* I gritted my teeth and felt my whole face burn.

"Why don't you go over and say something?" Sid suggested, interrupting me. "Man, I can't believe she'd rub it in your face like that. Who does she think she is?"

"Are you kidding?" I said. "No point in groveling. I have my pride."

When I looked away, I noticed Caroline sitting at the next table over with a trio of girls. How had I missed seeing her before now? She looked up and met my eyes.

I waved, and she smiled.

"Who's that?" Sid asked.

"Caroline Willis," I explained. "Brian White's ex. You know, the girl from the mall?"

"Oh, right," Sid continued. "You didn't tell me she went to this school, Jake. She's really cute."

"Well, why don't you ask her out? She's single, and I'm sure Brian White would love it."

"Yeah, right," Sid said with a groan. "Speaking of Brian White, wait till you see this new offense we're working on."

When Sid wasn't talking about girls, he was usually talking about basketball.

"Maybe I'll check it out at practice this afternoon," I said.

"Yeah, stop by. You'll get a preview of what we've got in store for Red Plains on Wednesday. We're looking good, man."

"Can't wait," I told him, resisting the temptation to look over my shoulder at Miranda again. *Don't give her the satisfaction,* I told myself. But the hamburger had lost its taste, and the french fries were cold. The food didn't fill the hollowness that came from knowing that Miranda was talking to another guy right now.

I looked over at Caroline again to take my mind off my own problems. As she talked to her friends I could tell it took an extra effort for her to appear cheerful. I knew what that was like. *She must not have gotten that message from Brian,* I thought. Well, after this afternoon everything would be cool. I'd talk to Brian White and straighten him out.

When the lunch bell rang, I picked up my tray. "I'll see you in the gym," I told Sid.

He had his mouth full of fries, but he nodded and mumbled one last comment about the team— it sounded like, "Bumble wart center court."

"You're absolutely right," I said as I took my tray to the drop-off counter.

Sid had ball practice last period instead of PE, and I had a study hall. I usually used it to write my columns for the school paper. Today when the final period came, I took a pad and pen and headed for the gym instead of the library.

When I got there, Sid and the rest of the Hillcrest Falcons varsity team were already on the court, in shorts and T-shirts, tossing balls around and doing warm-ups. I took a seat on the bleachers.

Sometimes I missed being part of the game, watching instead of having my hands on the ball. I'd played in the eighth grade and was also on the freshman team my first year at Hillcrest. But the fact was, I was only an average player; I was a better sportswriter. And having Sid hit harder, run faster, and jump higher than me at every sport got a little old.

As my dad told me, "Might as well go where your strengths are." But now, as I listened to the thud of a ball against the hardwood floor and the rush of running feet, I wished I was holding a basketball in my hands instead of a pen.

Then I spotted Brian White, and I remembered why I was here. He was tall, of course, and his arms and shoulders were corded with muscle. His short blond hair shone under the harsh lights; he had blue eyes and thin brows. Girls probably thought he was good-looking. But I wondered if they knew about the creep who lurked beneath his superjock exterior. He moved smoothly across the court, but as I watched I wondered what he thought about more: the team or his own moves.

When the team practiced a new play, a player named Turner prepared to pass the ball to Sid. But

Brian jumped across and grabbed the ball instead, hooking it neatly into the basket.

The coach blew his whistle. "Good shot, White, but you're out of position."

"I know, but I saw an opening," Brian said, grinning slightly.

Sid scowled. I could imagine what he'd say later. Just then another teacher came into the gym and waved toward Coach Edwards.

"Take a five-minute break, guys," the coach said, giving me my cue. I stood up and jumped down from the bleachers. At the side of the court Sid was taking a long drink of water.

"Want to say hi to the glory boy?" Sid asked, his tone sour. "That guy thinks he's the only person on the team, I swear."

"I know," I said. "And yeah, I do need to talk to him."

"Oh, man, you gotta be joking!" Sid hissed as I wandered past him and the rest of the team. "Watch yourself, Magee!" I heard Sid call from behind me. Where had White disappeared to?

I spotted him at one end of the row of bleachers, wiping his face with a towel. I walked over, not sure how he was going to react. Was he going to pick up where he left off?

"Hey, Brian?" I said hesitantly. "I'm Jake Magee. I write the sports column for the *Hillcrest Herald*."

No response. "Uh, 'scuse me, Brian?" I tried again.

Brian looked up. "What?" he asked, seemingly looking through me. I waited for him to pounce off the bleachers and begin strangling me, but he just sat there, staring blankly.

He doesn't remember me, I realized. *He doesn't remember that I pushed him Saturday. It probably doesn't even matter to him. Has he forgotten about breaking Caroline's heart too? Is that something else that doesn't matter?*

Suddenly getting an apology out of Brian didn't seem worth the effort. And the thought of patching things up between him and Caroline was out of the question. I had no choice but to get the interview I didn't really want.

"Want to give me a quote for the paper, Brian?" I asked cheerfully.

"Oh, sure," Brian said, looking interested right away. He tossed the towel back onto the bench. "You can say that I'm in top form for the game this Wednesday with Red Plains. Hey, you going to do a feature on me?"

"Should I?" I asked, trying to keep my tone even.

"Rising star, second-best shooting stats in the area, shadowed by college scouts, you bet," Brian boasted, flashing a wide grin. His eyes were a deep blue, and he puffed out his broad chest when he smiled.

"The city paper had me on the front page of the sports section twice this year," he continued.

"I guess it's hard to keep all that from going to your head, huh?" I said. But sarcasm was wasted on this guy.

He nodded. "But I try to stay humble."

"And the girls—I guess they're impressed?"

"You better believe it." He grinned and lowered his voice. "I have to fight them off, know what I mean?"

"I know what you mean," I said, though I didn't, of course. Did Caroline realize what a big head Brian had?

"In fact," Brian added, "I see a couple of admirers right now. They hang around the gym, hoping to see me."

I heard footsteps on the hardwood floor and turned quickly, half expecting to see Caroline. But the first girl who approached was taller than Caroline; her sandy hair was streaked with blond, and her lashes were heavy with clumpy mascara. She wore bright lipstick, and she blushed when Brian looked her way. The second girl was shorter and plumper, with dark hair. Both waved as Brian walked closer.

He put his arm around the tall girl's shoulders, and she leaned closer to whisper something to him. I was relieved when the coach blew his whistle and Brian had to sprint back onto the court.

How could Brian prefer this girl—these girls—

to Caroline? He was obviously looking for quantity, not quality. This guy had no class.

The nostalgia for my old days on the court had quickly disappeared. I didn't want to be back on the team for even a second.

The tangy scent of spaghetti sauce greeted me when I got home from my after-school job at the kennels. My mom had changed her business suit for sweats, and I saw a trace of tomato sauce on her cheek as she stirred the big pot on the stove.

"Smells good," I told her.

"We're ready to eat," my mom said. "Change out of your work clothes, please. You're covered in dog hair. You'll make your sister sneeze to death." She looked at me closely. "You okay?"

"Sure," I said. The aroma of garlic and basil almost made me forget all my problems.

When I got back to the kitchen after changing, everyone else was already there. "We were going to wait for you, but the smell was too tempting," my dad said, licking his lips. Nodding, I sat down and began stuffing my face while Kristen complained about the substitute teacher she'd had in science class.

"She told me to be quiet, and I wasn't even talking," she said, dipping her bread into the marinara sauce.

My mom looked at her, and Kristen shook her head. "I wasn't talking, honest. I was just answering

40

Sonya's question. She wanted to know if Jake is still available. She thinks he's cute."

"As if I'd look at a twelve-year-old," I said, frowning at my sister. "And don't tell the whole world about the state of my love life."

"Not the whole world," Kristen said earnestly. "Just Sonya, and Jennifer, and Cynthia, and—"

I groaned.

"Don't talk about your brother, and don't talk in class, period," my mom said dryly. Turning to me, she added, "I'm glad to see that you have your appetite back, Jake."

I looked down at my plate, which was now pretty much empty. "I've, uh, been busy today," I said.

"Does this mean that the Miranda thing is definitely over?" my dad asked, glancing at me over his glasses.

I remembered that in a rash moment, I'd sworn—out loud—that I would never be happy until I found a way to win Miranda back. "No, not exactly," I said, lifting my chin. "But I've got other things on my mind."

Everyone stared at me. Even Kristen was silent, and my dad raised his brows.

"It's almost Christmas," I tried to explain. "Haven't you always told us: Think about others, not yourself? Catch the holiday spirit? Well, I'm doing that—sort of." I realized that if I told them about Caroline, they'd get the wrong idea. I decided to tell them instead about how I was buying gifts for a needy kid.

"I'm impressed, Jake," my mom said when I was finished.

"Thanks," I said. I hoped that would keep them from bringing up Miranda—at least until after Christmas. Because if they could forget about her, then maybe so could I.

FIVE

I SPENT THE next half hour staring off into space. Caroline had done so much to make me feel better, and I wanted to do the same for her. So I decided to set her up with somebody. But the only available guy I knew was Sid. I definitely couldn't picture the two of them together.

What did girls look for in guys anyway? I guess if we knew that, all our problems would be solved.

As I headed for the kitchen I passed Kristen's bedroom and glanced inside. Music pounded from the stereo, and a clutter of clothes, magazines, paperback books, and assorted hair thingies covered the bed and part of the floor. Kristen herself was on the cordless phone, as usual.

"And then I said to Sandra—" She paused to look at me. "Go away! This is private."

But I was staring at a glossy magazine cover. "Can I borrow this for a minute?"

"What for?"

"It's, uh, for a school assignment. I need to check out some ads."

"Okay," she said. "But don't cut anything out without asking me first."

I tucked the magazine under my arm and went downstairs to pour myself a glass of milk. Back in my room, I glanced through the pages, shaking my head at some of the features—everything from hairstyles and eating disorders to dating advice and posters of rock stars.

I looked at an earring-wearing, tattooed singer with purple hair. Would Caroline would be impressed with this guy's fame and cool clothes, or would she like someone more down-to-earth? Caroline would prefer a normal guy, I decided. I flipped over to another page, and the article caught my eye. WHAT DO GUYS LIKE ABOUT GIRLS? the headline read.

Snickering, I skimmed over the article, which basically told me everything I knew already. But there was a list printed in a sidebar that stopped me dead in my tracks. It read:

Just what, exactly, makes up the perfect guy? According to our perfect-guy poll, he should be:
1. *Nice*
2. *Intelligent*
3. *Sensitive*
4. *Funny*
5. *Good-looking*

That all looked pretty realistic to me, but it was awfully general. I needed to know specifics; no use setting up an indoor type of girl with an outdoorsy guy or an animal lover with someone who was allergic to pets, like my sister, or worse, didn't even like animals to begin with.

I needed to do more primary research, as my history teacher liked to say.

I thought about calling up Caroline, but I didn't have her phone number. How many Willises were in the book? I went back down to the kitchen to check and found half a column of them. I didn't even know her parents' first names.

Besides, the thought of calling her up out of the blue just didn't seem right. Some guys, like Brian White, probably had all the confidence in the world when it came to calling girls—any girl. Maybe that comes with a big ego. Me, I was pretty deficient in the phone department.

Could that have affected my relationship with Miranda? Maybe I didn't listen to her as much as I should have. Maybe I couldn't find the right things to talk about on the phone—whatever that could possibly be. What a depressing thought.

Just then my dad came into the kitchen and poured himself a glass of milk, taking a cookie from the jar. He offered me one. "Finished with your homework already?" he asked, giving me a concerned look as I leaned against the counter with the open phone book in front of me.

That sounded like a Dad-type hint. "For tonight," I mumbled through a mouthful of cookie. I closed the phone book with a sigh. Calling Caroline was out of the question. But talking in the lunchroom wasn't.

"What's wrong with you?" Sid asked me the next day at lunch. "You haven't heard a word I said. And you hardly talked to me this morning in the weight room."

"She's not here," I muttered.

Sid groaned. "Miranda's at the table in front." He twisted to point her out. There was laughter from her table. "Man, she just doesn't quit, does she?"

Oh, Miranda. I didn't even turn around and look to see which guy she was sitting with today. "Sure, rub salt into my wounds," I said. "Kick me when I'm already down and the ref's not looking."

"You're making no sense," Sid told me. "As usual."

"Look, Sid, I'm trying to find Caroline," I told him. "I need to ask her something."

"What sort of proposition will you be making?" Sid asked wickedly.

"Not what you think," I retorted. "It's far too civilized to ever cross your fevered brain." Spotting Caroline on the other side of the cafeteria, I headed over to her table.

Caroline waved. "Hey, Jake," she said cheerfully. "These are my friends Stacey, Nancy, and

Caty. Guys, this is Jake Magee, star *Herald* columnist."

As I said hello to Caroline's friends I realized I hadn't gotten a close look at her since Saturday. Her eyes were puffy, as though she'd been crying for days. *I wonder if she's feeling any better than she looks,* I thought. *She could really use some cheering up.*

"Sit down, Jake," the girl named Stacey said. "We don't mind if you join us."

"No, thanks. I just had a quick favor to ask." I turned to Caroline, who now looked more curious than anything else. "I was wondering, if you're not busy, if you could help me pick out the gifts for Kevin—you know, from the angel tree—sometime tonight?"

Caroline looked off to the side, thinking. "Ummm . . . okay. Yeah. I'll be at the volunteer table, but my shift will be over about an hour before the mall closes. Is that too late for you?"

"No, actually. I have to work until then anyway. Meet you at the table?"

"Sounds good," she said.

"Great. Thanks," I called over my shoulder as I walked away.

"What was that all about?" Sid asked when I returned.

"Just saying hi."

"Man, that White is some idiot. Are you going to pay him another visit at practice today?" Sid asked, scooping up the last of his taco.

"Can't. I've got to do some work at the kennels." I decided not to tell Sid any more than that. He just couldn't believe that a guy and a girl could be just friends. Why set myself up for torture?

A cocker spaniel with sad eyes watched me through some wire mesh. "Cheer up," I told him. "I bet the girls think you're gorgeous."

When I spoke to him, he lifted his ears and yipped. He pushed his nose into the fence, and I reached over to stroke his silky head.

"Right," I told him. "Maybe I need longer hair and a wet nose, huh?"

I slipped him a doggy treat and he wagged his tail. I heard a sharp bark behind me.

"Hey, Riley," I said to the big collie across the way. "I need some advice. What does it take to fix a broken heart?"

Riley howled mournfully.

"Yeah. Beats me too," I said, taking off the heavy brown apron I'd put on over my clothes. I rarely bothered wearing it, but today was different. Even though I'd been in the doghouse lately, it was no use meeting Caroline covered in hair and smelling as if I belonged there.

There was a light dusting of snow on the ground that night as I made my way to the mall. I didn't have my own car yet—and considering how much money I made, it would be a long time before I did.

But my parents were pretty good about lending me their spare car—a 1992 Acura—when I needed it.

"Ah-choo." I grimaced. I'd splashed on some cologne I'd found in the bathroom at the kennels to try and erase the doggie smell, but it had made me sneeze about fifteen times. I hoped it'd end soon.

"Hey, Jake," Caroline greeted me when I got to the volunteer table. "I got here a little late, so I need to stick around for a few more minutes. Is that okay?"

"Fine," I said. "No rush."

"Great. There's a chair," she pointed out, and I dragged it over to where she was sitting.

To break the silence, I asked, "How did you end up being a volunteer?" as I sat down.

"My mom is part of the committee, and she said they needed more helpers. I thought it was a good project." Caroline paused. "My family adopts an angel every Christmas."

I started my mental list of things to look out for when I tried to set Caroline up. *Volunteer work, charities, stuff like that.*

As I watched Caroline work I noticed that she didn't seem as unhappy as she had earlier that day. She seemed more relaxed, more cheerful. "How's it going anyway?" I asked.

She sighed. "Not bad. When I'm here, everything seems okay. But when I'm at school, I . . ." She sighed. "Just the idea of running into Brian makes me want to drop out."

"You're lucky that you don't eat the same lunch as he does. Miranda takes second shift too, and it just kills me to *not* look at her. I want to see her face so much, but it's next to a different guy's every day."

Caroline shook her head. "Maybe she'll come back to you, Jake. Once she figures out what she's missing. You never know."

"I hope you're right," I told her. "I really do."

After Caroline signed up one more gift giver, she was finished for the night.

"Okay, let's go," she announced. "Did you bring the sizes?"

"Sizes?"

"The clothing sizes?" she asked patiently. "They're printed on the back of the angel cutout."

"Oh, yeah. I've got it somewhere." I found my wallet, took out the piece of paper, and showed it to her.

"See," Caroline pointed out, "this has his clothing and shoe sizes to help you."

"Clothes? It has to be clothes? Can't I buy any toys?" I imagined a six-year-old ripping open his present and how I'd felt at that age about receiving new clothes instead of something more exciting.

Caroline laughed. "Sure, but remember, clothing is a necessity. Toys are for fun."

"Fun is important too, especially when you're only six," I said firmly.

"You're right. Okay, let's make a plan. How

much can you spend?" Caroline asked briskly.

I told her, and Caroline nodded. "That should be more than enough. I bet you worked hard for that money."

"I have an after-school job at the Hillcrest Kennels," I explained. "Ah-choo!" I hoped I wasn't about to begin another sneezing attack. I felt like my sister when she's around cat fur.

"Oh, really?" Caroline asked as we started walking. "What do you do there?"

"I do a lot of cleaning, but I get to feed and groom the dogs too. It's a fun job mostly, except when I have to clean the dogs' pens. Do you like dogs?"

"Love them. We have a West Highland white terrier, Happy. Two cats too," she added.

"I wish we were that lucky. My sister would sneeze if a hamster moved in three doors down," I told her. "That rules out any pets in my house."

Caroline laughed. "That must be awful. I can't imagine living in a house without pets."

By this time we'd reached the largest department store in the mall. The children's department was on the second floor. Caroline led me to a display of jeans.

I fingered the stiff, new material, then pulled out one pair. "They're so small," I protested.

Caroline looked at my angel cutout again. "It says size eight."

I found a size eight and shook my head. Still

looked small. "I guess I've forgotten how little a six-year-old is," I told her. After that I picked out a warm red woolen sweater and a pair of snow boots, then paid for all of them.

"Okay," I announced. "Now I buy him something just for fun."

We headed toward the toy department, and on the way we took a detour through sporting goods. I paused long enough to touch a shiny new ski on a display rack. "Do you downhill ski?" I asked Caroline.

"Well, I tried it last year. I loved it," Caroline answered. "My family took a winter vacation in Colorado last January."

"I've always wanted to learn," I told her as we looked over the display. "My uncle taught me how to cross-country ski, but I haven't done any downhill skiing."

"It was fun, after I figured out how to stay upright for five minutes." Caroline giggled. "I fell into every snowdrift in two counties, I think."

Animal lover, outdoor type. At least I was collecting some good information. She was really talkative; it made my mission a lot easier.

"Let's go find those toys," I suggested.

"I know a shortcut," she said, pulling my arm. "This way."

I wasn't sure where Caroline was taking me, but as we passed the escalators I saw that we were heading for a department I didn't want to pass by.

"We're almost there," she said, running on ahead. She didn't even notice when I stopped in front of the display case with the gold heart pendant in it. The diamond sparkled, mocking me.

We love each other. That's everything to me.

The words echoed in my head, making me want to reach out and smash the glass in the case. My heart started beating as if it would burst out of my chest.

So this is just what you've been avoiding, Magee, I taunted myself. *The hard truth—staring you in the face. That pendant would be around Miranda's neck if she still loved you. But now it's there, waiting for some other guy to buy it and put it around some other girl's neck.*

I stroked the glass of the case as though it were Miranda's slender neck encircled with the delicate gold chain. *Face the facts, Jake. Ever since you met Caroline, you've been playing games. Caroline doesn't need you—just like Miranda. Why can't you be a man and admit it?*

"Jake?" I heard a soft voice behind me calling. A hand on my shoulder, a slight pressure on my arm. "Hey, Jake, are you okay?"

I turned to see Caroline, her face full of concern. Genuine concern. "Jake, what's wrong? You look like you've seen a ghost."

Rubbing my face with my hands, I calmed myself down. "In a way I have," I said quietly.

"Was that—" She pointed at the case.

"It was going to be," I replied before she could finish.

She smiled, nodded, and patted me on the back. "I understand," she said. "Do you want to keep shopping?"

"Sure," I replied with a nervous laugh. "Might as well get it over with."

Caroline really understands what I'm going through, I told myself, *better than anyone else I know. This isn't about ignoring my feelings or being selfish or selfless. It's about making this Christmas a happy one for somebody who deserves it.*

I shook my head, trying to sort everything out, but I still felt a little confused. Because deep down I still hoped that someone would do the same for me.

"How about this?" Caroline asked, holding up a toy spaceship covered in flashing lights. "This is pretty cool. Or maybe this?" She pulled out a giant plastic lizard with a gaping mouth. "He manufactures his own slime," she read. "Oooh, gross. Come on, Jake, pay some attention, okay? How do you like this?"

Caroline and I had gone through row after row of toys. I was still a little spaced from before, but Caroline was wrong: I *was* paying attention. It's just that nothing grabbed me.

"How many more toys do we have to look at, Jake?" Caroline asked, waving an ElectroSuperGlider

Truck with g-force capacity in front of my face. "What's wrong with this one?"

"It'll break in about five minutes. Doesn't anybody make normal toy trucks anymore?" I asked. "You know, those sturdy yellow ones. . . ."

"They do," Caroline said. "All you had to do was ask." She led me over to the next row, which had lots of good, solid yellow toy trucks to choose from. Just the sight of one made me feel like a little kid again.

Six years old. I could just picture Kevin varooming the biggest one.

"This is it," I decided, grabbing the biggest truck from the display.

The lights blinked, and I looked around in surprise.

"They're closing the store," Caroline said.

"Shoot," I muttered. "I was going to get these wrapped and then take them over to the booth. Now I'll have to bring them back later."

Caroline glanced at her watch. "Hurry, take the truck to the register. I'll hold the other bags."

When I came back, we found the last open exit and slowly walked out to the parking lot.

"Thanks a lot for your help," I told her. "I've never had so much fun shopping. Usually I hate it."

"It's for a good cause," she said. "That makes a difference."

"Oh, yeah," I agreed. "Absolutely."

"If you have any more questions," Caroline said,

"just give me a call." She took a pen from her purse and wrote her number on my brown paper shopping bag.

"Thanks again for coming with me," I told her.

She nodded. "Oh, there's my mom. Bye, Jake."

"See you," I called as she hurried to the car. I had found the perfect presents for Kevin—now Caroline was next on my Christmas list.

SIX

"WHO'S THE NICEST guy you know?" I asked Sid in the school parking lot on Wednesday morning.

"Come again?"

For a straight-A student, Sid isn't always so fast on the uptake. "I said, who's the nicest guy you know?"

"Why?"

"Suppose you wanted to introduce a really nice guy to your sister," I tried to explain as we walked through the front doors of the school and hit the crowded hallway.

Sid worked his way around a trio of giggling girls and then stared at me. "I don't have a sister. Your sister's only twelve. Your parents would never let her date yet."

"I know that," I said patiently as we reached our

lockers. I dropped my backpack and opened the locker door. "I only said, 'suppose.'"

Sid pulled out a couple of textbooks, wrinkling his forehead as he thought. "Gary Lankin, he's okay."

"Does he have a girlfriend?"

"Yeah, I think so." Sid banged his locker shut.

I could feel myself frowning. "You're no help."

I realized I'd have to find some likely candidates on my own. In geometry class I looked around the room, wondering which guys deserved to have a chance to meet a nice girl like Caroline. I looked at a guy sitting at the front; what was his name? Tony, that was it. He was quiet in class and polite to the teacher.

But as I watched, the girl behind him leaned forward and whispered in his ear. She put her hand on his shoulder, and Tony reached up and squeezed it. Tony grinned and the girl giggled, and in my head I crossed off his name. I was trying to mend a broken heart, not break any new ones.

When the class ended, I followed the stream of students out into the hall and saw a tall guy with shaggy blond hair straightening a crooked poster and retaping it to the wall.

BRING CANNED GOODS AND NONPERISHABLE FOOD TO THE BASKETBALL GAME TONIGHT, it read. HELP AN UNDERPRIVILEGED FAMILY HAVE A HOLIDAY DINNER.

I'd seen the sign before but barely noticed it. I

walked up to the tall guy. He wore a T-shirt with Save the Rain Forest printed on the front, and his green eyes met mine squarely. *He seems like a pretty cool guy,* I thought briefly.

"That's a good project," I said. "Who's in charge?"

"Me," he said. "Well, it's the science club, actually, but I'm the chairman of the food drive. Are you coming to the game?"

"Sure," I said. "I never miss a game. I'm Jake Magee."

He had his hands full, so he nodded. "Danny Erickson."

"Wait, didn't you organize a charity auction when that freshman's house burned down last year?" I asked, remembering an article from the school paper.

He nodded again. "His family didn't have insurance; they were almost out on the street. But the Red Cross helped them out, and we raised over a thousand dollars."

A cool guy for sure, I thought. *I bet Caroline would really like him.* Then the next bell rang, and he pushed the roll of tape into his pocket and picked up his books. "See you at the game."

Now I had a likely candidate. When I met Sid in biology, I demanded, "Know anything about Danny Erickson?"

"He's okay," Sid said, opening his textbook. "Why do you ask?"

"Just checking."

As Mr. Coombs wrote *mitochondria* on the board Sid rolled his eyes.

"What the heck are you up to?" he whispered. "You're either running a secret recruiting drive for the FBI or setting up your own dating service."

"More like the latter," I admitted, tapping my pencil on my notebook. "But keep your mouth shut, Halleman. You're supposed to run interference for me, not trip me up."

"But—"

"Mr. Magee, Mr. Halleman. Please, fellows, this is not social hour."

It was about the hundredth time this month that Mr. Coombs had to tell us to keep it down, but this time I was actually glad he did. The last thing I wanted was to tell anyone my plans and have Caroline talked about all over school. So I decided to keep Sid in the dark, at least for now.

At lunch, I picked the meat loaf special, and when Sid had filled his tray, we headed for the seating area.

I saw Miranda right away and tried not to stare. As I turned away from her I happened to notice Caroline sitting with her friends.

Sid and I put our trays down on a nearby table. "Back in a sec," I told him, and walked over. "Hey, Caroline, how's it going?"

"Okay," she said, putting down her fork.

"Though I don't recommend the meat loaf."

"Too late," I told her. "But I know the secret." I leaned forward and told her, in a stage whisper, "You just have to kill it with ketchup."

Caroline laughed. "I'll remember that."

"Hey," I said, "did you know they're having a food drive at the game tonight?"

Caroline nodded. "I saw the posters."

"Would you like to go and help out? I have to be there anyhow to write my column. I could pick you up," I suggested, thinking that way, I could make sure she met Danny.

Her expression was hard to read. "You want me to go to the game with you?"

"Uh, yeah," I said, wondering how to make my intent plain, but not *too* plain. If she figured out I was trying to set her up, her pride might be hurt. "I thought, two brokenhearted souls need a little distraction, right?"

"Well, sure, the game would be fun," Caroline agreed, but she still looked a little unsure. "I live just south of the mall."

She wrote her address on a paper napkin, and I tucked it into my pocket. Caroline's friends started giggling, but I ignored them. "I'll see you about six-thirty," I said. "Don't forget the food for the charity drive."

"Right."

I walked back to our table and found Sid staring. "What was that all about?"

"I asked Caroline to go to the game with me," I told him.

Sid set down his carton of milk. "What's going on, Jake? I didn't think you'd be ready to move on so soon."

"I'm not moving on, Sid. There's nothing between me and Caroline," I said, picking up my fork and poking the thick slice of meat loaf. I opened my packet of ketchup. "It's not a date or anything. Trust me."

"Are you using Caroline to make Miranda jealous? From what I've seen of Miranda lately, that might work," Sid said, his tone cynical.

"Hey, I wouldn't do that to anybody; for sure not to Caroline," I protested. "That would be too low."

"So what gives?" Sid pushed aside his plate and concentrated on a slice of apple pie.

"Promise you won't tell anyone?" I asked.

"Promise," he said firmly.

"It's not a date. I just thought I'd help her get back in circulation. If you saw how hard White was on her, Sid, maybe you'd understand," I explained.

"Oh," Sid said dryly. "You think that taking Caroline to a *basketball game* will help her get over *Brian White?*"

"Well, she *did* say she'd go," I said. "She's no coward. Besides, I'm going to introduce her to Danny Erickson. The rest should take care of itself. They'd make a great couple, you know?"

"Okay, Matchmaker Magee, if you say so." Sid sounded skeptical. "And what does Caroline think you're doing?"

"Hey, I told her we're two people with broken hearts," I responded. "She understands. Everyone knows how I felt about Miranda—how I *still feel* about Miranda. Including Caroline."

"Right."

"I'll see you at the game. Make sure Rylee keeps his mind on the defense tonight," I told him, ignoring his too knowing look.

Sid brightened. "You bet. Coach has a special pep talk planned, I think. We're going to be hot tonight; I can feel it." Sid snapped his fingers.

"I hope you're right, but keep that defense alert," I told him before attempting to actually *eat* today's main course. "I'll be getting it all down on paper," I mumbled, trying to chew through a mouthful of tough meat loaf. "Hope we run over them like a steamroller."

Sid chuckled. "Me too. Gotta run and check in with Coach Edwards. Give that meat loaf a decent burial, okay?" He picked up his tray and headed for the drop-off counter.

"Basketball game," I muttered to myself. "Way to go, smart guy." I couldn't believe that I asked Caroline to go watch her ex-boyfriend play basketball—and probably flirt mercilessly—for a couple of hours. *But she* did *say yes,* I reminded myself. That was a good sign; she was probably ready to get over him.

Too bad that's not the case for me, I thought as Miranda's laugh echoed in my head. *"You're so silly,"* I heard her say. But I refused to look up from the table, hoping that it was only the memory of her voice I was hearing and not the real Miranda saying it to some other guy.

"I need to borrow the car, Dad," I called as I heard him come home from work. "There's a game tonight."

"Okay. You'll have your homework done before you go, I take it?"

That was Dad's standard deal. I nodded.

"I'm leaving at six," I added.

"Why so early?" He had been glancing through the mail, but now he looked up at me over his glasses.

"Uh, I'm picking up someone," I told him.

"A girl? You've got a date? Good for you. It's time you stopped moping around," my dad said with pride in his voice.

"It's not a date," I protested. "Just a friend who happens to be a girl, that's all."

"Fine. I'm all for friends, male or female," my dad agreed, straight-faced. But I recognized the twinkle in his eye.

Parents. Why did they always seem to think they knew everything? Like I couldn't be friends with a girl? I grabbed a banana from the bowl of fruit on the counter and went back upstairs to attack the books.

At five-thirty I closed my textbooks and took a

quick shower. I wanted to look nice, but definitely casual. I decided on my favorite jeans and an olive-colored sweater. And I dabbed a little Polo behind my ears and on my neck for good measure. After I got dressed, there was a familiar knock on my door. "Come in." I groaned.

Kristen peeked around the door. "You going out with a girl?"

"No, an armadillo," I told her.

She stuck out her tongue and stomped off.

I'd already filled a bag with cans and boxes of food, letting Mom okay what I took from the pantry. I picked up the bag and took the keys off the counter.

Dad was watching the evening news in the family room.

"See you later," I said, snagging my jacket.

"Hope it's a good game. Have fun with your 'friend'," Dad replied with a grin.

"Funny, funny," I called over my shoulder as I walked out to the car.

As I rang the Willises' bell I realized just how calm I was. If this were a date, I'd be as nervous as the cat that had been put into the dogs' row at the kennels by mistake. But tonight I didn't have to worry about saying or doing the wrong thing. All I had to do was introduce Caroline to Danny Erickson. I smiled easily when the door swung open.

"Hi, Jake." Caroline pulled the door wider, and I stepped into the entryway.

She looked really nice in a red sweater and khaki slacks. Maybe Miranda *would* get a little jealous if she saw us together, I thought briefly. Then I pushed the thought away. This was about helping Caroline, not getting revenge.

"This is my mom," Caroline said. "Mom, this is Jake Magee."

"Oh, hi, Mrs. Willis," I said, shaking her hand. She was an older version of Caroline, a little plumper but still pretty. Her smile was friendly.

"Nice to meet you, Jake. You two have fun. Caroline, don't forget your gloves or the food you wanted to take for the food drive."

"I've got everything right here, Mom," Caroline responded, slipping on her jacket and picking up a shopping bag.

We walked outside into the frosty air, where our breath hung in faint clouds whenever we spoke.

"She still thinks I'm six years old," Caroline said, almost whispering. "At least she didn't remind me what time I have to be home. Parents!"

"Tell me about it," I told her as I opened the passenger door.

"Look," Caroline said as we walked into the gym. "There's the food drive table."

I spotted Danny Erickson seated behind the table, and I led Caroline over, donations in hand.

"What's up?" I said, nodding to Danny. "Oh, Danny, this is Caroline Willis," I added.

He nodded. "Yeah, we've met before. Hi, Caroline." He gestured to all the food. "Thanks, guys. This will be a big help to a hungry family."

"Looks like you're hauling it in," I said, glancing at the cartons overflowing with cans and boxes.

"We took in over ten boxes at Thanksgiving," Danny told us. "That's when we decided to do it again at Christmastime."

Another bunch of students came up behind us, and Danny turned to them. How could I give Caroline a chance to talk to Danny? I had an idea.

"You need any help packing these up after the game?" I asked. "Caroline and I would be glad to help."

Caroline looked at me in surprise, then nodded. "Sure," she agreed.

"Yeah, thanks," Danny told us. "We'll start about eight-thirty, if you want to lend a hand."

"That was nice of you," Caroline told me as we walked toward the bleachers. "People who think about someone besides themselves are rare, don't you think?" She glanced over at the Hillcrest bench, where Brian White was talking to Coach Edwards.

"I know what you mean," I told her. "Danny's a good guy."

Maybe this was going to work after all!

We found seats halfway up and sat down to

watch our Falcons practice. When the guys ran out onto the court, I kept an eye out for Sid. As he shot some practice baskets he looked loose and confident. *Go, Sid,* I thought, *looking fine.* Then I looked over at Brian White as he jumped to dunk the ball hard into the basket. He spun around and gestured at the crowd to make some noise. But just then a glimpse of long blond hair farther down the bleachers made me forget my disgust at White, and everything else.

Miranda. Wearing a tight lavender top that made her curves look even better than usual. Her smooth hair was pulled back behind her ears. A dark-haired boy sat beside her, flirtatiously stroking her back. I felt heat run through my whole body.

I gritted my teeth, hard. I had to look calm, had to keep it all inside. The urge to groan out loud came over me, but I pressed my lips together firmly and looked over at Caroline. She stared blankly at the court, not even noticing me. The game had started without my realizing it, and I could see out of the corner of my eye that she was following Brian's every move. I knew how bad she felt. Why was I putting her through this?

On impulse, I reached over and squeezed her hand.

She looked at me in surprise and flushed, looking almost confused.

I dropped her hand, but I gave her a friendly grin. "You okay?"

"Sure," she said, lifting her chin. "Absolutely."

She had guts, no doubt about it. *Good for her,* I thought as I turned my attention to the game.

The Red Plains Raiders were an even match for our Falcons. To my satisfaction, White's game was off completely, and he missed several easy shots. When White fouled out in the fourth quarter, Caroline scowled. But I couldn't tell if it was because she was unhappy to see him go or if she was disgusted with his flashy moves on the court.

Sid was solid throughout the night, and after White fouled out, his game really came together. In the end the Falcons won by thirteen points.

After the final buzzer I yelled, "Way to go, Halleman!" Sid grinned up at me, then stopped at the edge of the court to talk to a tall girl with curly ash blond hair.

I turned to Caroline. "Are you ready to help with the food drive?"

"Sure," she said, smiling. She didn't look too upset by the game; another good sign. We got up from the bleachers and made our way back to the food drive table.

Danny and two other members of the science club were loading the food into cartons. He waved at us to join them. "My pickup is outside; the food goes in the back."

"Why don't you help Danny fill the boxes," I suggested to Caroline, figuring they could get in some conversation as they worked. "I'll carry the cartons out to the truck."

A chunky freshman motioned for me to help him with a heavy carton of canned goods. As we lifted it and lugged it out to the truck I hoped my back would survive all this charity work.

The air was frosty as Caroline and I walked out to the car after all the food had been loaded. Snow was piled around the edges of the parking lot; the powdery white walls were nearly chest high.

"You cold?" I asked.

She shook her head, but I stepped a little closer so that I could block the wind. "Danny's a nice guy, isn't he?" I hinted.

"Yes, he is," Caroline agreed. "In fact, he's dating one of my friends."

"Ohhhh," I said slowly. *Think fast, Magee.* "Um, I guess she's a lucky girl."

"She is. She's really happy," she said vacantly.

Did *every* nice guy in this school already have a girlfriend? I'd wasted a whole evening pointing Caroline toward a guy who was already committed. And I'm sure she didn't appreciate my shoving the fact that her friend had a boyfriend in her face.

I had to do better than this.

But as we talked about the game during the ride to her house, I was relieved; she didn't seem upset at all. She even joked, "If Brian got points to match his ego, he'd really run up the score."

When we got to Caroline's house, I walked her to the door.

"I had fun tonight," Caroline said, loosening the scarf around her neck. "Thanks for asking me to go."

"I'm glad," I said. "See you tomorrow, I hope."

She hesitated a moment, looking up at me, then opened the door and slipped inside.

One down, I told myself. But I wouldn't be so easily discouraged. Somewhere out there, the perfect guy for Caroline was waiting.

SEVEN

"'NICE' WASN'T A winner," I mumbled to myself as I walked into geometry class the next morning. "So let's try 'intelligent.'"

I looked around the class, trying to identify the really smart guys. Unfortunately it was a small group.

There was Jason Morris, a tall, good-looking guy, but he already had a girlfriend; I'd seen them together in the halls. Who else? Ed Feltner? He was a smart aleck, and he always smelled like an old tennis shoe; Caroline deserved better. Sid was pretty smart, but I knew he was too much of a crackpot for Caroline.

Witzmiser. That's it, the Whiz. This guy was so smart that he scared the teachers. He wasn't in any of my classes, though. Even though he was only a junior like me, he was already taking calculus and other courses with the senior elite. He was super-smart—Caroline would be totally knocked out by him. Where could I "casually" bump into the Whiz, with Caroline along, so that they could meet?

When I looked at the bulletin board before last period, I found the perfect opportunity. There was a chess club meeting after school; the Whiz was a champion chess player, I'd heard.

Sid came up behind me. "Wanna head over to the weight room?" Basketball practice always started later on the day after a game, so today Sid had last period free, like I did. We'd usually shoot hoops or work out.

"Sure," I answered automatically.

We headed to the locker room. During gym class all the guys were supposed to wear the same thing: T-shirts and gym shorts in our school colors, yellow and black. But for casual workouts we could wear whatever we wanted. I changed into a well-worn R.E.M. T-shirt and a pair of University of Michigan sweatpants I'd cut off at the knee.

"Arms or legs today?" Sid asked as he pulled on a T-shirt with Falcon Power printed on the front.

"Legs," I said, tying my high-tops. "You ready?"

"Ready," Sid said, leading the way out of the locker room.

As we headed to the weight room I spun around when I heard, "Hey, Jake!"

"Hey, Caroline," I said, giving a little wave. "What are you doing over here?"

"Just getting out of gym," she said, shifting her books to her other arm. She looked a little flushed, and I could tell she had just freshly sprayed on some perfume. "Last night was fun, Jake," she said.

"It was," I agreed, feeling very conscious of the small holes in the front of my T-shirt. "You know what? I need to check out the chess club meeting after school for my sports column. Want to join me? It would be, um, different."

Caroline laughed; she had a nice laugh, not too high-pitched. "Why not?" she said. "Where should I meet you?"

"At the library's front entrance," I told her, picking at one of my frayed sleeves. "The club meets in one of the study rooms there."

"Okay, I'll see you at three-thirty," she said.

Satisfied, I headed into the weight room. Sid was already doing leg presses. "Hey, Sid," I asked. "Does Witzmiser have a girlfriend? You take senior physics with him, don't you?"

"That guy?" Sid made a face and let the weights fall with a loud *clank*. "I don't think he knows what girls are. Always has his nose stuck in a book—or a chessboard."

"Maybe it's time he found out," I suggested, warming up with some stretches. "Man cannot live by intellect alone." I remembered Miranda's clear blue eyes and sighed.

The Whiz should take a good look around him, I thought. *He'd see more than math equations and chessmen.*

"Magee," Sid said, sitting up and giving me the fish-eye. "Maybe you shouldn't be trying to set Caroline up with somebody. Would you want your love life managed for you?"

"If someone managed to get me back together with Miranda," I retorted, "yeah, actually, I would."

"Of course," Sid muttered, going back to his reps. "I should have known. Do you think that by making Caroline happy, you'll be happy?"

"Give me a break, Sid," I shot back. "As if you'd know."

We worked out in silence until the last bell rang. I headed to the showers. "See ya, Sid."

"See *you,* Samaritan," he replied dryly.

I spotted Caroline's yellow turtleneck from down the hall. She was leaning against one of the display cases that framed the library's entrance.

"Hi," I said, running my fingers through my towel-dried hair. "Hope you weren't waiting long."

"Nope," Caroline answered. "Where's your notebook?" She looked at my empty hands.

"What?" I blinked.

"Aren't you taking notes for your column?"

"Oh, that, sure." Fortunately I always kept a

small pad in my back pocket. I pulled it out and showed it to her.

Almost fumbled the ball, Magee.

I waved her toward the back of the library, where the study rooms were. When Caroline wasn't looking, I snagged a pencil that someone had left on one of the study carrels.

The chess club had already set up inside the biggest study room. It was a small group, but they had enough members to man—or woman—five boards. Caroline and I made our way to the side of the room, where we could slip into chairs and watch.

Each table had a small timer, and when it buzzed, one of the players would reach out and push a piece to a new square. Witzmiser sat bowed over his board like a skinny, injured halfback, and when his turn came, his arm moved with an abrupt, jerky motion. Behind his glasses he looked a little like Trent Reznor, and he wore a leather jacket with a Harley emblem.

"The basketball game was faster," I murmured into Caroline's ear.

I could smell just a hint of her perfume, something flowery and sweet. She was trying hard not to laugh.

"Think if I lobbed a pawn into the wastebasket, they'd all rush to the end of the room?"

She barely stifled a giggle, and the corners of her eyes crinkled.

I hoped the Whiz would appreciate just what a big favor I was doing for him.

"Ten-minute break," someone called.

I stood up and nodded to Caroline. "Come on, let's talk to a few of the players."

I walked straight across to Witzmiser and introduced myself, then Caroline. "I understand you're pretty good at chess," I said.

"Pretty good is a vague assessment," he told me crisply. "I ranked third in last year's state tournament, and this year I expect to move to the first position."

"Not bad," I said. "Why don't you explain some of your moves to Caroline while I get a camera. I need to take some shots when the break is over."

Caroline raised her brows, but she turned and listened patiently while the Whiz launched into an explanation of his strategy.

I edged my way through the other tables, heading for the door. On my way I bumped into another player as she stood up from the table.

"Sorry," I muttered.

The girl was short and chunky, with dark hair cut close to her cheeks. "I don't recognize you—are you a new club member?"

"No, I'm Jake Magee," I told her. "Sports editor and columnist for the school paper. I'm—"

"And you're doing a piece on the chess club? That's great," the girl interrupted excitedly. "I'm Mary Lou Kosemira. Did you know that I took third place in the last district tournament? Whiz took first, of course, but I've only been playing for six months. Would you like an in-depth interview—you know—rising star of the chessboard and all that?"

"Uh, maybe later," I said, suddenly reminded of Brian White. Not all the egos were confined to the ball teams, I decided.

But the rising star was off and running. "Let me tell you about the gambit I used in the winning game," she said.

I looked over her toward the door—and freedom. "I've got to go get a camera," I muttered to Mary Lou as she reeled off chess moves.

"Oh, you're taking pictures. Sure, I can finish my story later," she agreed.

I ducked out the door and found the librarian in her office. "Ms. Whitman, can I use your camera for some shots of the chess club?" I asked. Ms. Whitman was the newspaper adviser, and she always had a loaded camera that reporters could borrow for school events.

"Of course," she said, unlocking one of the drawers in her desk. "Nice to see that you're spotlighting one of the less traditional sports activities, Jake."

Great. Now I *really* had to write something about the chess club. I took the camera reluctantly and headed back to the chess meeting.

As I walked by one of the other study rooms I

got a glimpse of a familiar head of long blond hair. I paused—I couldn't help it—and glanced inside.

Miranda and several other girls were making posters and cutting out large cardboard snowflakes. As I hesitated in the doorway Miranda looked up and saw me.

"Jake!" she said in surprise. "What are you doing here?" Then she saw the camera. "Oh, is this for the paper?"

I walked inside, drawn like an ant to a picnic basket. I had to remind myself that she wasn't mine anymore. But I couldn't help looking.

"Maybe," I said slowly. "What are you working on?"

Miranda held up a large snowflake. "We're the decoration committee for the Winter Formal, of course."

"Of course," I muttered. The Winter Formal, the one big dance of the semester and the one I'd already bought two tickets to before Miranda decided she wanted her freedom back. I could have been dancing with Miranda, holding her tight against me, feeling the brush of that golden hair against my cheek as we swayed to the music. The thought of it made the pain return with full force.

But Miranda was still speaking. "We've been working hard every day after school. We want this to be the best dance yet. Are you going to take our picture?"

The other girls looked up eagerly, then concentrated on the cardboard in their hands, as if it didn't matter.

Miranda smiled up at me. How could I say no?

"Sure," I said. "Let me find the right angle."

I moved to the side of the room and tried to put together a good shot. And if Miranda just happened to be in the center of the picture—well, she was so beautiful that the camera just naturally gravitated to her. I had taken a couple of shots before I remembered I had to get back to the chess club.

"Got to go," I told Miranda hesitantly. "I'm sure your decorations are going to turn out great."

Miranda's left cheek dimpled, and I felt myself go weak. "Don't forget to vote for Snow Queen on the night of the dance, Jake," she called as I turned for the door.

I was glad she couldn't see my face. As if I would go to the dance without Miranda—it would only be extra suffering. What would be the point of watching her dance with another guy all night?

At least you got a few casual words with her, I reassured myself. I walked quickly back to the chess meeting on air.

The look on Caroline's face jolted me back to planet Earth. She was still side by side with the Whiz, and her expression was horribly strained. I tried to wave at her, but Mary Lou grabbed my arm.

"Now, about that chess ploy I was explaining—"

I hastily scribbled some notes and finally struggled back to Caroline and the Whiz.

"I understand you won the last district tournament," I said to Witzmiser.

"That's right." He looked at the clock on the wall. "Time for game two."

"Don't you want to give me a few comments about it?" I asked.

He'd already turned back toward his board. "She'll tell you." He nodded toward Caroline. "I explained it all to her."

"Did he ever," Caroline whispered.

"Sorry I left you with the Whiz," I said as we walked away, and I meant it. Witzmiser obviously wasn't the right guy for Caroline. Another good idea shot down.

Caroline rolled her eyes, but then she grinned. "It was *educational*," she said with a light laugh. "Anyway, I have lots of info for your column."

I made some notes as she repeated what she could remember, and I took several snapshots. I even got Caroline in one, convincing her to be the "interested spectator." Then she and I left quietly.

When I dropped the camera off with Ms. Whitman, she nodded. "Deadline for your column is tomorrow, remember."

"No problem," I replied. "For some strange reason, I have more than enough material this week."

Brian White wanted a feature in the paper, did he? Fine. When I got home, I typed up my sports column, following my chess club profile with a burning analysis of White's poor showing at last night's game, including the brief interview I had with him on Monday. After his boast that he was in "top form," I made some not-so-subtle comments about the dangers of overconfidence. *There,* I thought, that *should make him happy.*

"Look out, Brian White," I muttered as the column printed out. "The pen is mightier than the basketball."

EIGHT

"HOW'D IT GO with Caroline yesterday?" Sid asked as we rode to school the next day.

"Oh, the Whiz was a wipeout," I told him. "I have to find someone else. You know any sensitive guys?"

He gave me a funny look. "Excuse me?"

"For Caroline, stupe. I don't know any either. What the heck does it mean—sensitive?"

He opened his mouth, and the gleam in his eye told me that the remark he was about to make would not go over well with either his parents or mine.

But when Ms. Whitman stepped between us and asked for my column, Sid had to swallow his wisecrack. After I handed it over, Sid and I continued to our lockers.

Sid looked at me carefully while I pulled out my books. "Speaking of Mr. Sensitive, are you sure Caroline realizes that *you're* not interested in her?"

I almost dropped my math book. "What? Me? What are you talking about?"

"You've been hanging around together, haven't you?"

"Yeah, here and there, but they weren't dates. We're just friends."

"You sure she knows that?" Sid picked up his backpack.

I stared at him. "Of course she does."

He shrugged, and suddenly I wasn't as confident as I tried to sound. I had to swallow hard.

"We're just friends. She knows that. I'm trying to help her find a guy who's right for her. You said yourself that Brian White is a jerk. I couldn't encourage her to go back to him."

Sid still looked skeptical.

"I'm doing her a favor, okay? She doesn't know that, and I don't want her to."

"Seems to me she might think *you're* the one who's after her," Sid argued, slamming his locker door. "I tried to tell you before, remember?"

"I—uh—I—" The warning bell saved me, and I turned away and headed for class.

Caroline *did* realize we were just friends, didn't she? I'd never said the word *date* to her. But I couldn't help thinking: *Yeah, Magee, you just keep asking her to hang out with you. What do you call that?*

Caroline waved and smiled at me the second I walked into the crowded cafeteria with my food. I panicked and forced myself to smile back, setting my tray down abruptly on the nearest table.

Sid almost crashed into me. "What are you doing?"

"Eating," I said, taking my seat. "Just your normal, average upperclassman eating lunch with his friend. The *male* friend, not the *female* friend. No real difference, see?"

"You're losing it," Sid said. "I'm not the one you need to explain all this to." He sat down beside me and took a swig of Coke.

I bent over my pizza. I refused to walk over to Caroline. I didn't even look her way. I was afraid to look up at all.

Was she expecting me to ask her to the girls' basketball game tonight? I didn't want her to think I was asking her out; it was Friday, after all. But if I didn't talk to her, would she think I was avoiding her? After her horrible breakup, the last thing she needed was another rejection.

I'd only wanted to help Caroline, not set her up for another disappointment. If I messed this up, how would I ever explain it to her? She'd never forgive me, and I'd lose a good friend.

It had all seemed like such a good idea at the time. What happened?

★   ★   ★

I decided to stay home over the weekend. My parents were pretty surprised that I didn't go out Friday night, especially since I should have been covering the game. But I told them I wasn't feeling well enough. Which was more or less true.

"You're not going out tonight either?" my dad asked on Saturday night, peering over his glasses.

"No," I said abruptly, giving the log in the fireplace a sharp jab with the poker.

"How are you feeling, Jake?" my mom asked. "You're not coming down with something, are you?" She touched my forehead lightly. "Why don't you take some vitamin C?"

I shook my head. "No, thanks. I'm feeling better." Physically, at least. Vitamins don't do much good for a guilty conscience.

"What's wrong, Jake?" Kristen asked me later as I drove her to her friend Cynthia's house for a sleepover. "You're all quiet today. You didn't even get mad when I dropped the box of Christmas ornaments on your foot."

"I'm fine. I wish everyone would leave me alone," I snapped.

"I just wanted to help," she said, her tone injured.

"Trying to help can get you into all sorts of trouble," I muttered. Seeing how hurt she looked, I added, "Sorry. Really, I'm okay. I've just got a lot on my mind."

She nodded. "I don't like to see you sad," she

said as we pulled up to her friend's driveway. I could feel her staring at me, but I refused to respond. All I wanted to do was go home, crawl under the covers, and go to sleep. So that's exactly what I did.

When I got to the kennels on Sunday afternoon, I was greeted by the bark of a big red Irish setter. I opened the door of his pen and went inside. The dog thrust his head under my hand, and I patted him, stroking his wiry fur.

"What's the matter, Red?" I asked. "Your owner's coming to pick you up soon. You shouldn't have run away again, you know."

Red whined as if he knew I was scolding him.

"If Mr. Riggins weren't nice enough to take you in every time you wandered off, you'd be in the city pound or roaming the streets getting into trouble," I told him. "Better count your blessings."

He made a low, happy sound in his throat as I rubbed his head and neck and scratched behind his ears. His tail swung madly back and forth.

Red had a lopsided, drooling grin and an incurable wanderlust. He seemed to spend half his time away from home, and since his owner was an older man with arthritis who couldn't walk easily, I'd volunteered more than once to go looking for the big dog.

He wagged his tail even harder and stood up,

bracing his front legs against my chest. I rubbed his head.

"Looks like you've got a fan," someone behind me said.

I turned in surprise to see Caroline standing outside the mesh door. She was holding the leash to a slightly shaggy Westie. The dog's dark eyes gleamed at me from beneath her dusty white hair, and she yipped at the big setter inside the pen. Red came over to investigate, and the two dogs touched noses through the wire mesh. Red whined, and the smaller dog made more yipping noises.

"Are they going to fight?" Caroline looked alarmed.

I grinned and shook my head. "Red's harmless," I assured her. "They're just making friends."

Sure enough, the two dogs whined and wagged their tails happily.

I came out and closed the door to the pen behind me, pushing Red back inside. "What are you doing here?" She looked different—her hair was pulled back in a braid. I'd never seen her wear her hair anything but straight and loose.

"Our dog, Happy, needs a trim," Caroline explained. "So I decided to take her to the expert dog groomer." She tried to pull her dog away from Red. The Westie resisted, straining against the leash, and I bent down to pet her. Happy forgot about Red, for the moment at least, and licked my hand.

I grinned sheepishly as I stood up. "Expert, huh? You should have seen what I did to the first poodle I had to clip."

Caroline raised her brows. "Bad?"

"Try to imagine a poodle with a mohawk—all the way down to his tail," I told her as she tugged at the leash again. When Happy decided to follow, we walked back to the grooming shed. "The owner eventually forgave me, and the dog's coat did grow back."

Caroline laughed. Her hazel eyes glinted in the sunlight, looking clear and bright. *Why was I feeling anxious about talking to her?* I wondered. *Everything's under control. There's no tension at all. She's relaxed and easygoing, and so am I. No problems here.*

"Now, Happy, this is Jake," Caroline announced, gesturing to her dog. "I told the woman in the office I was a friend of yours, and she said you could squeeze us in now."

"Yep. No problem." I looked down at the Westie. "Hi, Happy." The little dog wagged her tail, then plopped herself down on the floor as I turned on the water in the big tin tub.

"You're going to bathe her too?" Caroline asked, watching me take out the dog shampoo and clean towels.

"Comes with the trim," I explained. I wrapped a rubber apron around me and offered one to Caroline. "In case you want to watch without getting drenched."

Laughing again, she took the apron. When the tub was half full, I gently picked up Happy and lowered her into the warm water.

The dog was pretty calm about it, twisting her head to watch as I wetted her down and rubbed in the shampoo. In a few moments she looked like a bright-eyed, creamy mop.

"I saw Sid today at the library," Caroline mentioned as she leaned on the other side of the tub. "He and Shelley were over in the reference section."

"Shelley?" I asked as I scrubbed the dog's fur. Sid hadn't mentioned a Shelley. Was this something new? "What does she look like?"

"She has blond hair, short and curly," Caroline replied. "She's pretty tall. I think she's on the girls' basketball team."

"Oh, right," I said, trying to keep Happy from chewing on the plastic shampoo bottle. "I saw them talking at the game last week. I think they're just friends."

"Probably," she agreed.

"I mean, it's not like two people can't be friends, even if they are a guy and a girl, right?" I watched her face closely.

"Sure," Caroline agreed, reaching for the shampoo bottle as Happy tried to take another bite of it.

I smiled to myself. Caroline got the hint; she understood that we were only friends. After all, meeting each other over a soapy dog wasn't exactly the most romantic encounter, and neither was hanging out with the chess club.

Sid was way *off track this time,* I thought triumphantly as I reached for the spray arm to rinse the shampoo off Happy. She put out her pink tongue and tried to drink the spray.

"You're good with animals," Caroline told me.

"Thanks. Look out, wet dog alert!" I lifted the little dog out onto the mat and toweled her down quickly before she could shake off and drench us both. When I took out the large hair dryer that I used to blow the animals dry, Happy suddenly seemed *un*happy.

When I flipped the switch, she barked madly at the whirling dryer. I turned it off, then tried to calm her. "It's okay. It won't hurt, I promise."

Caroline petted the little dog, then we tried again, putting the dryer on its lowest and least noisy setting. Eventually I had the animal dry enough to trim. In a half hour Happy's dark eyes were no longer hidden under her shaggy hair, and the rest of her looked pretty good too.

"Nice job," Caroline said. "I guess you've come a long way since that poodle."

"Thanks," I replied as I fastened Happy's collar back around her neck.

Caroline snapped on the leash and headed up front to pay. "See you tomorrow," she said casually.

"Yeah," I agreed. "See ya."

I whistled happily as I headed back to work.

Now I knew that Caroline was okay with everything after all. I could tell she wasn't expecting more than friendship from me. As long as I wasn't misleading her, I would try one more time to find her a perfect match.

Maybe the third time would be the charm.

NINE

O N MONDAY MORNING the school building smelled like wax, disinfectant, and wet wool. The fresh shine of the floors was already marred by slush. I stepped carefully over a puddle to keep from slipping, then looked up at the posters on the wall.

The Booster Club was holding their annual Winter Carnival this week. There'd be special events every day, ending with the Winter Formal on Saturday night, when the Snow Queen would be crowned. Then school would be out until after New Year's.

I paused to examine one poster more closely. Tomorrow after school there'd be a snowball-throwing contest out on the football field. It sounded promising, especially because the master of ceremonies would be Wade Hamilton, the class clown. Would Caroline go for a guy with a sense of humor? As far as I knew, Wade wasn't going with anyone, and I'd overheard more than one girl say he was good-looking.

"There you are, Magee." Sid clapped me on the back. I'd given him an advance copy of my upcoming *Herald* column to read, and he waved it in his other hand. "You know how I feel about Brian White, but *jeez,* did you have to hit him so hard?"

"You of all people should *not* complain," I said, laughing. "White's had this coming for a long time, and I was more than happy to give it to him. His head is way too big for the team's good, not to mention his own."

"Yeah, but when this thing comes out, you'd better believe there's gonna be trouble," Sid warned.

"Who cares?" I replied. "I already got in one scrape with Brian White, and all he did was brush me off. I guess he thinks he's untouchable."

"Well, it's pretty harsh in black and white," Sid said, his eyebrows raised.

I turned back to the poster. "Say, Sid, what do you think of Wade Hamilton?" I asked, changing the subject.

Sid groaned. "When will you be done with this matchmaking business? This is getting old."

"Come on, help me out here."

"Wade's okay, I guess," Sid said. "He's sort of crazy."

"*Really* crazy or just occasionally weird?" I demanded.

Sid paused. "Occasionally weird, I'd say."

I translated that to "hilariously funny" and decided to check Wade out in the afternoon. Maybe he'd be the one for Caroline.

Caroline seemed pretty interested in going to the snowball-throwing contest when I stopped by her locker and asked her. Walking to the library for my last-period study hall, I tried to come up with ways to get her and Wade to meet. I was pretty much in my own world—so much so that when I saw Miranda standing in the hall by the library, I thought I was imagining things. But as I got closer I realized that it was no illusion. Miranda was there, and she was waiting for me.

For me.

I felt light-headed. Kids were standing around in the hall and talking, but the sounds were only a faint humming in my ears. Almost as a dare, I walked over to where Miranda stood and leaned my shoulder against the wall, facing her. She didn't move away. She only smiled and said, "How's it going, Jake?"

"How's it going with you?" I said, keeping my tone steady. No need to let her know that my heart was threatening to jump out of my chest. Miranda looked great, better than ever. She was wearing a short black miniskirt and a snugly fitting white sweater. Her lips curved into a perfect pout.

"Okay, magpie," she cooed, using one of the nicknames she had given me. "What's up with you these days?"

"Not much," I said. "Just keeping busy." *Busy trying to keep my hands off you.* But I wasn't going to tell her that, of course. This was the girl who had wanted her freedom. This was the girl who had dumped me.

But her next words almost made me forget my weeks of heartache.

"I've missed you, Jake," she said, smiling up at me.

"You have?" I shifted my books to my other arm. "You've had lots of friends around to distract you."

"Ever since I saw you the other day, I've been thinking," Miranda said, running a finger up my shirtsleeve. "It just hasn't been the same without you around."

The sexily pleading tone in her voice made me ache to grab her up in my arms and run for the nearest exit. But I wasn't quite sure where she was coming from. "Honestly?" I asked cautiously.

"Honestly, sweetie," she said. "I'm really sorry for what I said to you a few weeks ago. I wasn't—"

The last-period bell shrilled through the hallway, drowning out the rest of her words. There was a surge of noise and movement as everyone started heading for class.

"What was that again?" I asked after the bell finished ringing.

"Look, Jake," Miranda said, "I have a lot of things to tell you. How about you meet me at my locker right after class?"

"I'll try to be there," I said as coolly as I could, then turned away into the library before she could catch a glimpse of my reddening face. As Miranda walked away, my mind buzzed with possibilities. Why was she being so nice all of a sudden? Could it be true—had she really missed me, like she said?

Strategy, Magee, I was telling myself. *Use your strategy.* What strategy? I wanted to find Sid to ask him what I should do. But he was busy with practice, and besides, why did I need him to tell me what to do? I had dated Miranda for three months. If anyone knew how to handle this, it would be me.

My decision was to take my time getting to Miranda's locker that afternoon. No way would Jake Magee *run* back to any girl—certainly not one who'd left him flat. Plus, if she was willing to wait for me, I'd know for sure that she was serious.

As I turned the last corner before her locker Miranda was already standing there in her long wool coat, pouting. "What took you so long?" she asked meekly. "I was beginning to think you were blowing me off."

Me blow *her* off? That seemed hard to believe. "Sorry, Miranda—" I waited for her reaction. Her face remained sweetly sad. "I was just running a little late. What's up?"

"Go get your coat, sweetie, and meet me out front. I'll tell you all about it." She kissed the tip of her finger and tapped me on the nose with it before turning around and walking toward the main entrance.

I had passed the first test. "Yes!" I said quietly, lightly punching a fist in the air before running to my locker at top speed.

A fresh, light dusting of snow covered the sidewalk as I walked Miranda home from school. Her house wasn't too close—about twenty minutes away. But we used to take advantage of the moments we could be alone together when we were dating, and the walk to her house was one of them. We'd always take our time, stopping off in stores or for something to drink, or getting romantic at the playground in the park along the way. Some afternoons we'd draw the walk out for five, ten times as long as it needed to be.

Today the sky was already darkening as our feet crunched in the snow. I tried not to be aware of how close she was, how her shoulder brushed against my arm. I could once again smell the flowery perfume that haunted me on those sleepless nights after the breakup. I reached over and dared to take her hand, and she didn't resist. A cloudy breath escaped her lips, and she turned to me. "Jake, the whole reason I asked you to meet me—well, it wasn't what I said. I don't have a lot to tell you."

"You don't?" My heart sank. I braced myself, expecting her to tell me that she had found some-one else.

"No, Jake. Just one thing. I want—I want us to get back together again."

My chest filled with so much warmth, I was surprised the heat coming off me at that moment didn't melt the icicles on the tree branches. "Miranda, I don't know what to say."

"Then don't," she said, squeezing my hand. "Let's just walk."

We continued in silence until we got to the playground. Without a word we both turned and walked to the slide—our slide.

Our slide was a raised, square platform with a different slide coming down each of three sides and a ladder up to the fourth. Over the platform was an ornate metal roof supported by four posts. The paint was chipping, and it was a little dented, but it was all ours—or so we liked to think.

We climbed up the ladder and sat under the roof—a dry sanctuary from the snow-covered land-scape.

Miranda rested her head on my shoulder, and I put my arm around her. "Does this mean you'll take me back, Jake?" she asked quietly.

"Mm-hmm," I said, lifting up her knit hat to

expose her forehead. I kissed it, and she closed her eyes.

"Oh, Jake, I've missed you so much." She turned her face to meet mine. Finally we kissed, and I didn't want it to stop.

"Let's stay here awhile, Jake," Miranda said quietly as we took a moment to catch our breath. "I like it here."

"Me too," I replied, rubbing my thumb over the dimple in her left cheek.

She smiled.

The bus couldn't move quickly enough. I had to get to Sid's and let him in on the news. *Wait till I tell Sid,* I thought. *Wait till I tell—*

Caroline. A sinking feeling forced its way in, interrupting my bliss. Here I was, back with the girl I loved, and Caroline was still single and alone. I pushed the thought away by remembering my marathon make-out session with Miranda in the park. Soon the bus jolted to a stop, and I ran out and over to Sid's house, covering his front yard in about three strides.

"What's with you?" Sid asked when he answered the door. "You look like you just walked into a brick wall."

"I'm happy," I said, kicking a clump of snow off his front stoop. "You're not gonna believe it. Miranda and I are back together."

"Excuse me?" Sid asked, stunned. "But I heard she was dating a guy from St. Andrews."

"No way. She's dating me now."

"Let me get this straight, Jake. You took Miranda back?"

"She threw herself on my mercy, she apologized, she almost groveled," I told him shortly. "What do you think I am, totally brainless? Should I pass up my dream girl over a little injured pride?"

"Defensive, aren't you? How come you're acting so weird?" Sid asked. "You should be happy, not hysterical."

I leaned against the doorjamb. "This is what I want," I told him. "Just take my word for it, okay?"

Sid furrowed his brow in an exaggerated grimace. "Okay, okay. Look, we'll talk about this later. Gotta cram for physics. Take care of yourself, man. Don't have a heart attack over this."

"'Night," I said as Sid shut the door.

I walked back to my house. What an amazing day. The realization was still sinking in that Miranda was my girl once again—that my wish had finally come true. But part of me felt sad. Unsettled.

Maybe it was because of Caroline. Because Caroline was still alone, still sad, and I couldn't do anything about it.

TEN

"SO, JAKE, ARE we still on for tonight?"
Caroline's voice made me whirl around so fast, my locker door nearly dislocated my shoulder. It was Tuesday morning, and I was still reeling from the night before, so naturally I had forgotten that I was planning on introducing Caroline to Wade Hamilton after school at the snowball throw. I couldn't tell Caroline that I was dating Miranda again—that would be too humiliating. But how could I take another girl to the snowball-throwing contest?

I had to. That was it. I was stuck, and there wasn't anything else I could do.

"Sure, Caroline. Meet you . . ." Where could I meet Caroline without Miranda seeing us? "Meet you by the photography darkrooms right after the last bell, okay?"

"The darkrooms?" She laughed. "You're weird, Jake. Okay, fine. See you then."

What have you gotten yourself into? I asked myself. *There's only one way to get out of this. Get Caroline set up with Wade and get out. Do what you gotta do—just don't let Miranda know about Caroline. And don't let Caroline know about Miranda either.*

How weird was that? If I piled any more guilty feelings on myself, I'd collapse from the weight. *Just make it through this day, Magee,* I told myself, *and if you play your cards right, your commitment to Caroline will be over.*

By some miracle I had made it through the school day without any run-ins. I was able to steal a few quick kisses from Miranda out of everyone's sight. Miranda had a committee meeting during lunch, so I could say hi to Caroline without Miranda seeing me. Miranda was also going to be working on the decorations for the formal after school, so I knew I wouldn't run into her at the contest. Now I was waiting by the darkrooms in Hillcrest's least-traveled hallway. I made sure I got there early so I could wave Caroline through the fire doors for a speedy exit.

A female voice echoed down the hall. I walked out to see if it was Caroline, but I caught a glimpse of who it was and panicked. *Miranda!*

She was talking to two other girls, and they all

had their arms filled with poster board and containers of paint. *The art rooms,* I realized. *They're working on the decorations in the art rooms. How much of an idiot am I?*

Miranda caught me and waved me over. "Hey, Jake!" she called brightly, loudly enough to echo through the whole building. "Why've you got your coat on?"

"It's cold on this side of the building," I answered nervously, hoping she wouldn't ask why I was there. Her blue eyes were calm, but they did nothing to soothe the anxiety I was feeling.

"I'm glad I ran into you. Would you give me a hand here, sweetie?" Miranda asked.

Busted, I thought. What else could I do? "Okay," I blurted quickly, taking some of the materials and bringing them into one of the art rooms.

Over Miranda's shoulder I noticed a shadow approaching along the hallway. Caroline! I jumped over to the far side of the art room, and Miranda took it as a hint that I wanted to see her alone. She sauntered over as I heard Caroline's boot heels click down the deserted hallway.

"Hi," she cooed, kissing me on the chin. "Can I ask you something?

"Shoot," I said.

"There's a big skating party tomorrow night at the city rink, and I was wondering if you'd like to go. Everyone'll be there."

Miranda was asking me out! Wow. "I'd love

107

to," I said, and her face lit up. "I'll be sure to get the car."

"Pick me up at six-thirty?"

"Deal," I said. "Now I'll let you get to work here. Later." I gave her a fast kiss before darting out of the art room and down to the darkrooms at the end of the hall.

The sound of boot heels coming my way greeted me. I ran as quickly as I could toward Caroline as she raised her arm and waved. She opened her mouth to speak and I brought my finger up to my lips, signaling her to be quiet.

"Why?" Caroline whispered.

"Artists at work," I explained before leading her out the fire door.

We walked out into the frosty, crisp afternoon air. A booth had been set up at one end of the football field. Wade Hamilton, decked out in several layers of red thermal underwear, was doing a handstand on a platform about twenty yards from the booth.

I had assumed that Wade would be standing by and making jokes throughout the event. I didn't think he'd actually be the *target*. I glanced at Caroline. Maybe she wouldn't be impressed with him.

But she was grinning. "How does this work? Oh, I get it."

Members of the student council were at a table making loosely packed snowballs to sell for fifty cents apiece. Since Wade was generally well liked, no one was trying to make their own snowballs for free. Besides, there wasn't a lot of snow on the ground, and most of it had been piled up near the student council table. When someone's turn came up, they would have to stand in the booth and throw the snowball at Wade.

"There's one thing I don't understand," Caroline said. "Why would anyone want to pay fifty cents to throw a snowball at somebody?"

"You'll see. Wade has a special talent." I pointed toward him. "He's a really good guy, but he's just enough of a kidder to make you *want* to throw something at him—and pay for the opportunity."

Wade ran around, jumping and tumbling, evading most of the snowballs that flew at him. Wade was a varsity gymnast, and his skills were obvious.

"What's the matter?" he called toward the booth. "Can't hit a moving target?" He did another handstand on top of the platform. "Here. I'll try and make it easy for ya!"

A stocky freshman tossed a snowball his way, but Wade went into a roll and it sailed past, falling to the ground in a powdery burst.

"Hey, I haven't even worked up a sweat, guys," Wade called, back on his feet. "Who's next?"

"Want to try it?" I asked Caroline.

She was still smiling. "Why not?"

I bought a couple of snowballs and handed the first one to Caroline.

"Wow, at least this time it's a gorgeous girl!" Wade said. "My luck is changing."

Caroline flushed slightly. She took aim and tossed the snowball, but Wade was too fast for the slow-moving missile. He ducked and it flew past his shoulder.

"Sorry!" Wade called cheerfully.

Caroline shook her head. "You try," she said to me.

A moment ago I hadn't cared about scoring, but now suddenly I wanted to show Caroline that I had a pretty good throwing arm. Wade looked like he needed a little snow on his face.

I picked up the snowball and made a high throwing motion. Wade ducked. But I hadn't released it—not yet. When I did, it caught him low, a light smack in the face. He slipped backward off the platform.

Wade made a sputtering sound, then shook off the snow while the crowd roared.

Caroline turned to me, laughing. "Good shot!"

I tried to look modest.

Wade was up again, making funny faces. "Hey, come on. Is our school sportswriter the only guy here who can throw?"

He sure knew how to bait the crowd. Half a dozen guys hurried to buy more snowballs.

"Let's edge up along the side," I said. "I want to say something to Wade."

"Looking for a snowball-throwing trophy?"

Caroline asked mischievously, following me over.

We watched Wade jump and roll. He moved easily around the platform, and most of the next throws missed him completely. *These guys couldn't hit the side of a barn,* I thought.

We waited for a pause in the action, when two student council members hurried to shovel some more snow into a wheelbarrow.

"Hey, Wade, come over here," I called.

He jumped down from the platform and walked over. "Wade, do you know Caroline Willis?" I asked.

"No, actually," he said, reaching out a snowy, mitten-clad hand. "Hi, Caroline."

"Hi, Wade," Caroline replied. "So you're our class clown, I take it. You're pretty good up there."

"Except for the sneaky ones," Wade said, looking over at me. "Next time I'll pay you to stay home."

Caroline and I both smiled. "Just helping a good cause," I said.

"I hope we raise enough money," Wade agreed. "The gymnastics team needs—"

We never found out what new equipment the gymnasts were hoping to buy. Someone yelled, "Wade, incoming!"

Wade turned aside and ducked hastily out of the way of the huge snowball that was heading in his direction. It kept flying—straight into Caroline's

111

face. It hit her cheek with an icy *smack!* and snow flew everywhere.

Everything went quiet.

"Are you okay, Caroline?" Wade asked. "That wasn't an ice ball, was it?"

Caroline didn't answer.

"Oh, no," I groaned.

Wade, for once, was making a face that wasn't funny. "Wow, I didn't mean—s-s-sorry, Caroline," he stammered, in a rare loss for words.

Caroline shook the snow off her face and out of her eyes. "That's okay." She winced as she wiped her face with the sleeve of her coat. A few tears formed in her eyes, but looking at me, she began to laugh. I must have seemed even more horrified than Wade. "All for a good cause, right?"

The rest of the crowd started laughing too, and Caroline didn't seem to mind. She shook the last traces of snow from her dark hair. "Here, let's get out of the way."

"I'm sorry, Caroline, I shouldn't have—I didn't think—" I couldn't get my words out straight.

"I have to say that going out with you is never boring," Caroline said wryly, blowing her nose.

"Going out?" I stared at her, my stomach sinking. "What do you mean, going out?"

Caroline still had snow on her long eyelashes. She blinked, and the snow turned to ice. "I just meant, dates with you are full of the unexpected."

"But it's not a date," I blurted.

Caroline looked at me, her expression strange. "I know it's not a formal—what do you mean, not a date?"

"We're just friends," I said. "Like we discussed at the kennels. We're not *dating*."

"At the kennels? Oh, that. We were talking about Sid and Shelley. At least, I thought—" Caroline suddenly flushed.

"I can't ask you out, not on a date," I said, floundering. "I'm still in love with Miranda. I thought you knew that." What she didn't know was the fact that I would be going on a date with her tomorrow. How could I tell her?

"Excuse me?" Caroline's expression was as icy as the snowballs that were whizzing past us.

"I just thought that—"

"What do you mean, in love with Miranda? I thought she broke up with you! I thought you were trying to get over her! Why did you tell me all that stuff about broken hearts and how we had so much in common?" Caroline's hazel eyes flashed fiercely.

"I only meant—we did, we *do* have a lot in common. I knew how you felt, so I just wanted to help." I gave Caroline a pleading look, but she didn't seem convinced.

"You just seemed so upset," I continued, "and I didn't want you to feel so bad, that's all."

"I am *not* a charity case!" Caroline stamped her foot and almost slipped on an icy patch. Some kids started staring at us.

113

I reached out to steady her, but she jerked her arm out of my grip. "Of course you're not," I said desperately. "I like you a lot, Caroline, but we're friends, you know? I mean, after dating someone like Miranda—"

Caroline's face turned a bright red, and it wasn't from the cold. I knew then that I'd gone too far.

"You've lost your mind, Jake Magee, if you ever had one to begin with," she said angrily. "I'm *so* sorry I don't meet your specifications. What a shame! But let me tell you something. I *never* want to speak to you again. Is that clear?" She turned and stormed away before I could apologize.

Caroline was right. I *had* lost my mind. I was a total jerk. So much for helping Caroline out, so much for making her feel better. How could I have been such an idiot just now? I wanted to crawl under the bleachers and stay there forever.

When I turned to leave—*slam*—something cold and hard smacked me in the chest, followed with a softer, more powdery blast. It was a familiar sensation, one I hadn't felt since grade school.

An ice ball, with a snowball chaser. Just what I needed.

A roar of laughter went up from the crowd as I rushed to clear the snow from my jacket. I already suspected who the culprit was, but I wanted to find out for sure.

I noticed Brian White was bent over, laughing

harder than anyone else. He caught me glaring at him and made a face.

"Whoops! I tripped! It just flew out of my hand."

"Give it up, White. Ice balls don't make themselves," I snapped.

"No kidding. Well, it couldn't have happened to a nicer guy!" he sneered as the laughs got louder. As if he hadn't already made his point, he crumpled up a copy of the just released *Hillcrest Herald* and flung it at me.

My plans for Caroline were slipping away with the melted snow that dripped off my jacket.

What else could go wrong?

"You want to clean my face?" I asked a little cocker spaniel who was trying to lick my chin while I groomed him. I rubbed his soft head. "You should have been at school with me this afternoon. I had egg all over it."

When I was finished, I cleaned the dog runs, trying hard to block any and all thoughts out of my mind. Then I bathed a Doberman pinscher who evaded my towel and shook himself vigorously, throwing most of the water on me. By the time I was finished at the kennels, I was almost as wet as the dogs and definitely more depressed.

I felt like a total failure. The kennel was covered with Christmas lights and decorations, but the sight only made my spirits drop even lower.

Christmas—season of good will. *Bah, humbug*. What did I have to be happy about? I was back together with Miranda, but at what cost? I'd managed to hurt Caroline's feelings when all I hoped to do was help her out. When would she be calm enough to hear me explain? Probably never.

Ten minutes before the end of my shift I walked over to the receptionist's phone and dialed Sid's number.

"Yeah?" Sid answered.

"Hey, Sid, you busy?" I asked.

"What's up, Jake? Just hanging out, wrapping Hanukkah presents. No plans."

"Meet me at Little Nicky's in twenty. Can you do that?"

"Sure. Wait, is this about Miranda?" Sid had that *I-told-you-so* tone in his voice.

"Sort of. Listen, I'll tell you later," I said, hanging up the phone before Sid had a chance to say "See ya."

Little Nicky's was a small, family-run pizzeria on a secluded block near the kennels. It was Sid's and my favorite place to hang out. I'd never taken Miranda there; it seemed too personal, as though bringing her there would be like letting her look through my underwear drawer. It was sort of like a clubhouse for me and Sid, our home away from home.

As I walked in, I breathed a sigh of relief. It was

116

comfortable here, like a safe zone. Already I could feel myself depressurizing.

"Jake, how you doing?" asked Tino, the owner. "Long time, no see."

"Been better," I said. "But maybe a large half sausage, half meatball deep dish with extra cheese will do the trick."

"Let me guess—Sid's on his way," Tino said, and I nodded. "Coming right up."

As I took our usual booth and waited I realized that Tino was right. It *had* been a long time since I had been there—the last time was right after the breakup with Miranda. Had my life really changed that much since then?

"What's up with you?" Sid asked, interrupting my train of thought.

"Good news first or bad?" I asked.

"Uh, bad news, I guess," Sid responded, sitting down and pulling the ski cap from his head.

"I messed up with Caroline," I told him. "We had a huge fight yesterday. You know what? She *did* think we were dating." I shook my head. "I thought I had explained to Caroline that we were only friends, like you and Shelley, but it didn't come out right. I should've listened to you sooner, Sid. I feel like a complete idiot."

"Oh, man," Sid said, with a strange look on his face. "Uh, Jake, there's something I have to tell you. Shelley and I *are* actually dating. We have been for a few weeks now."

117

"What?" I sat up and glared at him. "I never see you two together. What's the big secret?"

"No secret," Sid said, looking uncomfortable. "I just didn't want to make you feel even worse—throw it in your face that I had a girlfriend, you know, when you were feeling so down. Hey, Magee, are you mad?"

I shook my head. "Nah. You and Shelley together—that's really great. How's it going?"

"Can't complain," Sid said, punching me lightly on the shoulder. "So what's the good news?"

"It's good. I mean *real* good," I began. "I'm going out with Miranda tomorrow night."

"*What?*" Sid exclaimed. "But what about the guy from St. Andrew's?"

"I think you heard wrong," I told him. "She's not dating anyone but me. We're really back together! Is that unreal or what?"

"Sounds unreal to me, all right," Sid said sardonically. "Miranda Thomas, Her Royal Highness, has changed her mind? Sounds to me like she's doing that every few minutes. Be careful," Sid said wryly. "'Weather vanes are always turning,' my granddad used to say."

"Watch it, Sid. She's serious about this. I knew things seemed great after school yesterday, but this is the best thing that could happen to me. She means it, Sid. I should know."

"Yeah, that's just it," Sid muttered. "You

118

should know. Sounds to me like you don't. Careful, buddy. Stick your neck out with her and she'll chop your head off. She's done it once before."

"Give me a break, Sid. Can't you just be cool about this?"

Just then Tino came to the table, holding one large half sausage, half meatball deep dish with extra cheese on a wooden board.

Sid gave me a glare. "Say, Tino, could you make that pie to go?"

"Yeah," I replied, returning Sid's look while I put on my coat. "Suddenly I'm not all that hungry anymore."

At home that night I tried concentrating on my math homework, but all I could see was Caroline's face. I remembered how crushed she had looked. She was already feeling wounded before I came along. Why hadn't I been more careful? Now she felt worse than ever, and it was all my fault. Some Christmas gift I'd given her.

I was half asleep when I heard my mother in the hall.

"Anyone want some hot chocolate?" she called.

"I do," Kristen said quickly. I could hear her bedroom door opening and her feet pounding down the stairs.

"Jake?" Mom asked. "How about you?"

She had that "I'll listen if you have something to say" tone in her voice. But tonight I just wasn't in the mood.

"No, thanks," I said.

I heard Mom head down the stairs, and I turned off my light. I had the feeling it was going to be a long night.

ELEVEN

*M*IRANDA LOOKED UP at me with sparkling eyes as we glided effortlessly around the rink. "Jake, you're everything to me," she whispered, her breath warming my ear. "How could I have ever let you get away? Nothing can keep us apart now." She squeezed my arm, and I pulled her even closer.

Every guy from our school was watching us. We were the perfect couple, and they were green with envy.

Sid winked at me and pointed toward the side of the rink. Caroline was sitting there alone, looking wistful. My happiness faded, and my grip on Miranda loosened.

You can't ignore Caroline anymore, I told myself. You've hurt her more than you realize. But in the meantime why couldn't I savor being in love

121

again? I reached for Miranda and held her as tightly as I could in order to shut Caroline out of my mind. . . .

I woke, pounded my pillow, and turned over, trying to shake Caroline out of my head and to dream of nothing other than Miranda.

"I need the car for a school skating party tonight," I told Dad at breakfast. "It's really important."

Mom glanced up. "I don't need it," she said.

Dad put down his mug. "Sure. What time's the party?"

"It starts at six. I'm—I'm taking someone."

"Date?"

I nodded.

"Caroline seems like a nice girl," Dad said, taking a bite of toast.

"Uh, no," I said. "Caroline and I are—were—just friends. I'm taking Miranda to the skating party."

"I thought Miranda dumped you." Kristen had come into the kitchen. "Did she take you back?"

"Who says *I* didn't take *her* back?" I demanded. "Who said she dumped me?"

"*You* did." Kristen reached for the box of cereal and poured it into her bowl. "That's all we've heard for weeks: how your life was over, how you would never date again, how—"

"Okay, already," I said. "I get the picture."

Me and my big mouth. Next time I was totally in the dumps, I'd have to remember not to spill my guts to my little sister.

"Better be careful. She'll dump you again," Kristen observed, pouring milk on her cereal.

"Who made you Dear Abby?" I demanded.

"*Someone* needs to help you out," my pesky little sister retorted.

"I don't need any help," I snapped. "I'm back with Miranda!"

Kristen rolled her eyes. *"Sure,"* she drawled sarcastically.

"If you don't mind your own business, I'm going to stuff that cereal—" I began.

"Have some toast, you two," Mom said quickly before I could make good on my threat.

The whole day seemed to be conspiring against me. The morning crawled by, slow as molasses. Sid was cool during the ride to school this morning, and at lunch he hardly said a word. Miranda was holding a committee meeting, so she ate with a bunch of girls and I couldn't even get near her.

As I entered my math class I happened to notice Wade Hamilton talking to Caroline in the room across the hall. *Probably apologizing for what happened yesterday,* I figured. *I bet he's doing a better job at it than I ever could.* Then her shoulders began shaking with laughter. She threw back her head and laughed some more.

She sure didn't seem upset. I was bewildered. Well, maybe she was just trying to show me that she was better off without me as a friend. I walked into class and concentrated on getting through pre-calculus—and the rest of the school day.

I didn't concentrate hard enough. I flunked a pop math quiz and left my English homework in my locker. Through it all I focused on the skating party. The night was going to be so wonderful that the awful day wouldn't even matter. But it was still a little hard to believe that Miranda and I were back together again.

To confuse me even more, the image of Caroline with Wade kept gnawing at me. On the one hand, I was glad to see her looking so happy; maybe she wasn't hurting as much as I thought she was. Still, something about it didn't seem right. She seemed to be laughing a little *too* hard. Maybe she was only putting on a show, trying to hide how sad she really was.

That thought made me feel even worse.

By the time I pulled into Miranda's driveway that evening, my mood had lifted so much that I was humming along with the car stereo. I had picked out a blue sweater—Miranda's favorite color—and combed my stubborn hair carefully. I had made a promise to myself not to let thoughts of Caroline interfere with my date, and it seemed to be working.

When I rang Miranda's doorbell, though, I was suddenly nervous. By the time the door swung open, my stomach was doing flips.

Miranda wore a soft pink sweater and a short, flippy white skating skirt over pink tights. She looked even more stunning than usual.

"Hi, Jake, come in. I have to get my coat. You know my mom," she said as her mother came into the hall.

"Hello, Mrs. Thomas," I said.

"How are you, Jake?" her mother said politely. "I hope you two won't get cold."

"We'll be fine," Miranda said. I held her parka while she slipped her arms into the sleeves. Then Miranda pulled on soft blue knit gloves and a matching cap that made her look even cuter. She grabbed her skates just before we headed out to the car.

"You look like a dream," I murmured as I opened the car door for her. She slid into the seat and smiled. I was hoping she would sit very close to me during the ride, like she used to, but she stayed on the far side of the car. I wanted to hold her hand, to put my arm around her shoulders, but it just didn't feel like the right time.

When we got to the rink, it occurred to me that I hadn't been on the ice much this winter. I glanced at Miranda, bent over as she put on her skates. I hoped that I wouldn't do anything stupid. But then I saw her light hair fall forward over her face. She looked like an angel, and all my anxieties disappeared.

Miranda looked up. "Ready?" she asked.

"Oh, yeah." I stood up too quickly and almost lost my balance.

Miranda swallowed a giggle. I slowly and cautiously held out my hand to her. She took it, and we made our way onto the ice.

Miranda was as graceful on the ice as a professional skater. She did a little twirl while I was still getting the feel of the ice beneath my feet.

"You're really good," I said.

"I took lessons for two years," she said, sliding into a smooth figure eight.

The sweater and short skirt emphasized her gorgeous figure, and I smiled. By this time I was feeling less awkward on my skates, and I offered her my arm. "Want to skate together?"

"Sure." She glided up to me, and we made a leisurely circuit around the rink, arm in arm. This was what I had dreamed about. The music on the loudspeakers was an old love song, soft and dreamy. Reaching over, I squeezed Miranda's hand and waited for her to respond.

"Oh—there's Jennifer," she said quickly. "I need to ask her a question about the decorating committee. Let's stop for a sec, okay?"

"Okay," I agreed. We skated over to the other side of the rink so that Miranda could talk to her friend.

Fragments of Miranda's conversation—"more silver glitter," "the photographer said," "not enough streamers"—floated by while I leaned against the railing and stared out at the ice. Suddenly I spotted Sid's purple parka across the rink. He was with Shelley.

I looked at Miranda, but she was still deep in discussion. "Be right back," I said—unsure if she'd even heard me—and took off across the ice.

Sneaking up behind Sid, I gave him no warning before I clapped him on the back.

"What?" He spun around, almost slipping, and I grinned.

"Surprise," I said. "What are you doing here?"

"I need your permission to go skating?" he said, giving me a quizzical look.

I laughed. Everything seemed a little funny tonight. "Great party," I told him. "It's nice to see you guys."

He glanced over at Shelley. "Shelley, this is my friend Jake. Jake, Shelley."

"Nice to meet you," Shelley said warmly.

"Same here," I said.

Shelley touched Sid's arm. "I'm just going to go tighten my laces. I'll be right back." She waved good-bye as she skated off.

"She's really terrific," Sid said, smiling.

"Take a look at Miranda." I pointed her out to Sid. She was still talking to Jennifer. "It feels so good to be back together again. It's almost like we never broke up, you know?"

"Oh, uh-huh. I can see how wrapped up in you she is." Sid's tone was wry.

"Hey, come on!" I said. "She's got a lot to do this week, that's all."

"I just don't want to see you moping around if the golden girl changes her mind again," Sid told me. "I don't think I could take any more of your grumbling."

"You're being a jerk, Sid," I warned.

"You're being a moron," he retorted. "And Miranda is going to chew you up in little pieces."

"What do you know?" I threw back at him. "You're wrong," I said stiffly. "You're wrong and you know it."

Sid shrugged and skated off toward Shelley, who was making her way out on the ice again. "I hope so. See you around," he called over his shoulder.

"Maybe," I muttered. "And with that attitude, maybe not."

As I skated back toward Miranda, Sid shouted one last thing at me. "If you want to see a *really* happy couple, Magee, take a look in the snack bar!"

I turned around to look at him, but he had already put his arm around Shelley and was leading her out onto the ice.

A really happy couple? I was trying to figure out what Sid meant by that remark when Miranda looked up, smiled brightly at me, and finally finished her conversation. "We'll talk about it tomorrow, Jennifer," she said as she took my arm.

The touch of Miranda's arm, the sweet smell of her perfume—I tried to enjoy the moment and put aside my frustration with Sid. How could my best friend not understand? Miranda and I *were* a happy couple. Weren't we?

As we skated in silence my anger began to disappear. I wanted to hold Miranda in my arms, tell her how I was feeling.

When I turned to face her, she abruptly let go of my arm. "*There's* Kara. I was wondering where she was," she said impatiently. "I'll be quick, magpie, I *swear*." Miranda gave me an apologetic look before she skated over to her friend.

I followed Miranda over. Kara was trying to show her little sister how to stop without falling down.

"Kara, hi," Miranda said. "Did you finish the decorations for the front table yet?"

Great. Why didn't they just call a committee meeting right here on the ice?

"Jakey, sweetie," Miranda said, placing the tip of her finger on my chin. "You know what I'd love more than anything?"

"Name it," I replied, hoping that her request didn't have anything to do with the decorating committee.

"I could really go for a hot chocolate."

"Uh—okay," I said. "You want me to get one for you?"

"I'll meet you in the snack bar in ten minutes," she promised. "This won't take a sec."

129

"Right." I stepped off the ice rink and made my way to the snack bar. By the time I ordered two hot chocolates, fifteen minutes had gone by. Miranda still hadn't shown up.

As I waited for my order I remembered Sid's words. A real happy couple in the snack bar. "Let's see what these two look like," I muttered to myself.

I turned and looked around the seating area. There were only a few silent pairs of underclassmen staring down at their tables. *Obviously on first dates,* I thought, snickering. *Sid doesn't know what he's talking about.*

But when my order appeared, a laugh rang through the snack bar. A familiar bell-toned laugh. Caroline!

I grabbed the two hot chocolates and headed out to the booths, not believing I'd missed her. I could see that there was one hidden booth in the far corner of the seating area that I hadn't noticed.

Caroline was there, her back to me, laughing nonstop. Sitting across from her, gesturing wildly, was Wade Hamilton.

My last attempt to set her up worked after all, I thought, feeling a little relieved. *Time to stop feeling guilty, Magee—she may be mad at you, but at least you found somebody for her.*

I briefly thought of going over and saying hi, but instead I took a sip of my hot chocolate and watched them secretly. Every once in a while Wade would reach across and touch Caroline's hand or

130

her shoulder. His eyes never seemed to leave her face. *Can't blame him,* I thought. *Caroline is a pretty girl.*

But as the minutes passed, I could feel my face burning a little. Caroline and I always had fun when we were hanging out together, but I had never seen her laugh as hard as she was laughing now.

On dates with Miranda, I sometimes felt like I was holding back a little, like I was afraid to be myself. Caroline didn't seem to be having that problem with Wade. How could she let him get so close to her so soon?

Caroline and Wade got up and left the snack bar. I watched through the window as they put on their gloves and went out onto the ice. I found myself giving Wade the evil eye, secretly hoping he'd fall and make a fool of himself. But then I remembered that Wade was the class clown. He already did that on a daily basis.

I had to admit that Wade skated like a pro. He led Caroline around the rink in an exaggerated tango; her sparkling grin never left her face.

Caroline was having the time of her life while I was sitting alone in the snack bar with two cups of cold hot chocolate.

This wasn't how I had imagined my perfect date.

When Miranda finally appeared, I waved, and she slid into the seat across from me. I pointed to her cup of cocoa, and she took a sip.

"Thanks, Jake." Then she grimaced. "It's cold!" She set the cup down and looked at her watch. "Oops—I have to go look for my mom."

"Your *mom?*" I said in surprise. "What do you mean? I was going to take you home when you were ready. We just got here."

"Oh, Jake." Miranda's eyes widened innocently. "I'm sorry. I forgot to tell you—I have to leave early. We're going over to my grandmother's tonight."

How could Miranda forget to tell me something like that? "You could have mentioned it before," I said, trying not to sound too annoyed. Miranda sighed helplessly. "But, um, do you want to get together again?"

"Sure," Miranda agreed. I helped her unlace her skates, undid my own, and shrugged back into my jacket. I stole one last glance at the rink. Wade and Caroline were on the ice, spinning around in each other's arms. I quickly turned away.

"Tomorrow, maybe?" I suggested as we headed for the front entrance.

Miranda looked thoughtful. "I have to go to the mall after school tomorrow," she said. "Why don't we go together?"

"Sounds great," I said, relieved.

The air outside the double doors was cold, but the moon cast a warm glow. I moved closer and put my arm around her shoulders.

Miranda smiled at me. "I had a lot of fun, sweetie, I really did."

I leaned in to kiss her. Just when our lips were about to make contact, she turned.

"There's my mom," she said, breaking away from me.

Sighing, I followed her to the car.

TWELVE

THE NEXT MORNING Sid decided to take off for school without me. It shouldn't have come as a surprise, considering our blowout the night before. At lunchtime I had decided to wait outside the cafeteria for him anyway, in case he wanted to talk. But when he sped right by me without even looking in my direction, I knew it was no use.

Miranda drew me out of my misery as she waved a pale-blue-sweatered arm in my direction. "There's an empty seat here." She beckoned from inside the cafeteria.

When I went in and sat beside Miranda, she gave me the most caring look I had ever seen. All my uncertainties about the night before slipped away when she touched me gently on my arm, giving it a little squeeze.

"You look nice today," she said, touching my

sweater. "Did you pick out blue because it's my favorite color?"

It was the first time she'd ever noticed that I had worn blue. But today it was completely by accident; in my morning confusion, I had thrown on the first things I could find. There was no way I could admit that to her. "Uh, glad you like it," I said.

She flashed her brilliant smile, then turned to one of her friends and discussed decorations for the Winter Formal. I ate my sloppy joe carefully, trying not to dribble any tomato sauce on my chin.

It's a lot easier eating lunch with Sid, I thought. But I threw the idea aside, remembering all the bad things he'd said about Miranda the night before.

Miranda suddenly got up. I blinked and wondered what I'd missed. "I'm going to a decoration committee meeting," she explained. "Say, sweetheart. Would you be able to help us put up the decorations at the hotel ballroom? It would be Friday, after school."

"Sure, glad to help," I replied, a little dazed by her sudden exit.

"Are we still on for this afternoon?"

"What?" I really needed to pay more attention.

"We were going to the mall, remember?" She looked confused, as if she thought I had forgotten completely.

"Can't wait," I said. "Meet you at the front entrance?"

She flashed a gorgeous smile. "See you

then," she called over her shoulder as she walked away.

With Miranda gone, I decided to sneak just a glimpse of Caroline. I scanned the room and soon found her sitting with Wade. He grinned as he talked; Caroline wasn't smiling back. But when he leaned close to her, she didn't pull away. What was wrong?

She rubbed her face abruptly. Was she crying? What had that clown done?

I stood up abruptly, then slowly sat down again. Whatever it was, Caroline wouldn't want my help; she'd made that plain. I'd meddled in her personal life enough already.

As I watched, Caroline got up and walked away. Wade followed her and placed his hand on her back. She turned around and leaned her head on his shoulder, and he put an arm around her.

If it was a fight, they seemed to have made up. But somehow that didn't make me feel any better.

"I'm sorry I couldn't get the car today," I told Miranda as we took our seats on the bus to the mall.

"That's okay," Miranda replied. I reached over and took her hand; it was as warm and soft as the contented glow of her face. I squeezed her fingers gently. She returned the pressure, and I felt my heart swell.

When we got to the mall, we walked past the

store windows, holding hands and talking. It felt just like old times.

As I looked toward the center court a distressing thought nearly stopped me in my tracks. I'd already spent all my money on the charity gifts. How could I buy a gift for Miranda?

I'd get another paycheck soon. Would that be enough? A girl like Miranda expected—*deserved*—a nice gift. I was so busy trying to come up with a plan that I didn't realize that Miranda was waiting for me to answer a question.

"Sorry, what?" I asked.

We'd stopped walking in front of a dress shop. Miranda stared wistfully at a pale blue dress, soft and flowing, in the window. It looked fit for a princess.

"That's the dress I wanted to wear," she said sadly. "It's not much fun making decorations for a dance I won't get to go to."

We both stared at the dress for a long moment until I nearly kicked myself for being so dense. "You d-don't have a date for the dance?" I stammered, finally taking the hint. I had two tickets for the formal at home; I'd bought them ages ago, before the breakup. I'd even reserved a tux at the rental shop and never had the heart to cancel it.

"Miranda, you know how much I wanted to go to the formal," I continued. "But we broke up. I never thought you wouldn't have a date . . . and then this week I guess I just wasn't thinking."

I paused, taking a deep breath. "Would you go with me?"

She smiled, all her sadness disappearing. "Oh, yes, Jake. I thought you'd never ask."

"Great," I said, grinning. I hugged her tightly. I wanted to kiss her, but the mall was crowded with people, and one little kid with a candy-streaked face was already staring at us.

"I'll come back with my mom tonight and pick up the dress." Miranda looked radiant. "I'm so happy."

So was I. *Finally*.

We drifted on down the mall, walking on air. Miranda stopped suddenly in front of a lingerie shop. "I need to go in here for a minute," she said.

I looked at the lacy bras in the window and turned away quickly. "Uh, I'll meet you when you're done. I'll be over at the pet store, okay?"

"Okay." She headed into the shop, and I walked down to the pet store, avoiding the center court. Caroline probably wouldn't be too happy to see me. Even if she was, what if Miranda walked by?

The pet store was my favorite place in the mall. I loved to watch the squirmy little puppies and kittens yawning and stretching in the front window. Inside, they had lots of fish and parakeets, and there was even a snake and a large parrot with scarlet wings. I hoped that when Miranda met me later, she'd want to watch the puppies with me, just like we used to.

I glanced idly over the notices posted on the bulletin board. There were announcements for a dog training class and an upcoming cat show. There were always signs posted about lost pets. I read them with sympathy: a white Persian, a German shepherd. The next notice made me stop and catch my breath.

LOST: FEMALE WEST HIGHLAND WHITE TER-RIER, ANSWERS TO THE NAME OF HAPPY. LOST NEAR THE VICINITY OF THE MALL ON WEDNESDAY. REWARD. CALL JAMES WILLIS, 555-1218.

That was Caroline's dog! No wonder she had been crying at lunch today—she must be so worried. That poor little dog was out there somewhere, cold and hungry.

I stared at the sign, thinking hard. Caroline and her family must have already searched for Happy. Where could she have gone? I wasn't sure how long I'd been standing there when I felt a hand on my arm.

"Hey, wake up," Miranda said playfully. I turned and saw her with a small shopping bag in her hand. "Are you through in here?" She spotted the large snake in a cage behind us and shivered.

"C'mere." I brought Miranda over to the front window and put my hand gently around her waist. "Look at that little guy there," I said, pointing to a Rottweiler puppy sleeping with a paw over his muzzle. "What do you think—Bruno? Or how about Rufus?"

I turned to Miranda expectantly, but she was looking past me toward the food court. "Sweetie, I'm starved. Can't we go get something to eat?"

"Okay," I said dejectedly, following her lead. Suddenly it didn't seem like old times anymore.

Miranda was almost finished with her ice-cream sundae when she pointed to my untouched chocolate shake. "Is something wrong with your drink?"

"Oh, no, it's fine," I said, picking up the paper cup. *Why don't you ask if there's something wrong with me—with us,* I thought, my head spinning. I knew that I was happy to be back together with Miranda—maybe *overwhelmed* was a better word. I knew things wouldn't be quite the same as before. We were just getting back on our feet. But there seemed to be a barrier between us that I couldn't get through.

Then I remembered the last time I had been at the food court—with Caroline. We talked so easily, so freely. And we hardly even knew each other. Still, when I left that day, I felt as though I had made a friend for life.

A friend for life. Did I ever make a mess of *that.*

Why did the idea of dating Caroline make me so nervous anyway? We were hanging out together, and we always had a great time, even though my motives were totally screwy. Why should I have been afraid of being with a girl I could laugh and joke with, feel completely comfortable with? That girl was Caroline—not the girl sitting across from me right now.

But I had just promised the girl sitting across from me that I would take her to the Winter Formal—I had made a commitment to her.

Kinda makes you think, doesn't it? I taunted myself.

Suddenly the stout woman next to me stood up to gather her two little kids. Her heavy shopping bag hit my arm, and my shake went flying. Most of it landed on Miranda's skirt and sweater.

"Oh, no!" Miranda jumped up and wiped at the mess.

I jolted out of my seat too, scrambling for a napkin. "I'm sorry, Miranda—that woman's bag—"

"*Un*-believable, Jake!" Miranda snapped. "Can't you be just a *little* careful?" She glared at the table, seething. She made a face as though she just remembered something, and out of nowhere she turned apologetic. "Sorry, sweetie. I know it wasn't your fault. But I *just* bought this outfit. Today's the first day I've even worn it."

"Well, maybe you should go home and soak it or something," I suggested. "At least, that's what my mom always says."

"You can't *soak* wool, Jake," Miranda told me dryly. "But I *do* need to get out of these clothes. Want to come with me?" She looked hopeful—and more than a little desperate.

"Sorry, but I, um, need to check in at the kennels." I hoped Miranda would forgive me for what I was about to do, because it was a lot more important than cleaning her sweater.

I had to make it up to Caroline.

THIRTEEN

"GOOD EVENING, HUMANE Society."

"I'm looking for a lost female West Highland white terrier," I told the woman on the other end of the phone. "She's been missing for a day now. Can you help me?"

"Sorry," the woman said. "We haven't received any Westies this week. It's supposed to be a cold night. I do hope you find her."

"Yes, ma'am," I said. "I do too."

I dialed the kennels next. Sometimes dogs who came in for grooming would wander by if they'd strayed from home, like Red did.

"Sorry, Jake," Mr. Riggins told me. "I haven't seen any terriers. Mr. Francisco gave me a call yesterday and said Red's out on the prowl again, but I haven't seen him either."

Red was up to his old tricks. I shook my

head. "Thanks anyhow," I said, hanging up the phone.

Suddenly I had an idea. *Red!* I remembered how Happy had responded to the big dog when she'd been at the kennels to get groomed. Had she run into the setter? It wasn't impossible.

Okay, that was a start. I didn't know Happy very well, but I sure knew Red's haunts. The only problem was, there were so many, and the wind was starting to get really cold.

When I got home, I ran up to my room and pulled on an extra sweater and a knit hat. I grabbed the leashes I had left over from an old dog-walking job and ran downstairs. My dad was working late, and the Acura was in the shop. I'd have to ride my mountain bike.

"Dinner's almost ready, Jake," my mom called from the kitchen. "Don't go out again."

"I have to, Mom. I'm looking for a lost dog. If it gets too dark, I'll never find her."

"But it's so cold," my mom said, sounding worried. "The radio said that the wind chill is—"

"I know," I said. "And these dogs could freeze to death. Look, I took my hat and some gloves too."

My mom sighed. "I'll put a plate for you in the fridge," she told me, shaking her head. "Warm it up when you get home. Be careful, and don't stay out too late."

"Later, Mom," I said as I zipped up my jacket and ran out the door.

Cycling along the side of the road, I could feel the cold pinch my nose. My fingers tingled. I lowered my head against the wind and pedaled harder down the ice-patched road.

I rode to Burger Barn, the nearest fast-food restaurant. When I went inside, the strong smells of burgers and fries hit me, along with a wave of warm air. The warmth felt good.

"Seen any stray dogs hanging around here?" I asked a guy behind the counter.

"All the time. What kind are you looking for?" he asked.

"A big red setter and a small white terrier, might be together," I told him.

"Hmmm." He stopped to wipe off the counter, then leaned across it. "Think I did see some dogs like that earlier today. The big red one tried to jump into the Dumpster, and I had to go out and yell at him."

"Did you see the terrier?"

"There was another mutt, smaller, but I don't remember what it looked like," he told me.

"Thanks," I said as I ran back outside, blinking as the cold air made my eyes water.

It had been nearly two hours, and there was still no sign of the dogs. I pedaled as quickly as I could, leaning into the icy wind. Darkness was deepening, and I was getting exhausted. *Maybe you should pack it up,* I told myself. *This was a stupid idea anyway. No matter how hard you try, Caroline is not going to give you another chance. Give it up, Jake. Forget it.*

Disheartened, I turned the bike around, letting the bike's headlight sweep over the darkness by the side of the road. I caught a flicker of movement at the edge of my vision. For an instant it didn't register.

"Red?" I called. "Red!" Nothing moved. *Just seeing things,* I figured. *An illusion. You should be used to that by now, Jake.*

Exasperated, I got back on the bike and pedaled toward a long brick office building. Then I heard a bark—real, not imagined. I sped up the driveway and toward the alley.

"Red!" I yelled, pointing my bike headlight into the pitch black of the alley.

There was a movement in the darkness, then the big setter loped forward into the light, his tail wagging and his tongue hanging out.

"Here, Red!" I called.

He came closer, sniffing the pocket of my jacket, which held a packet of dog treats I had brought along.

"I was hoping you'd have company," I said, giving him a treat. "Happy? Happy, come here!" I yelled.

148

Just when I decided that I'd been off base, I heard the scrabble of small feet on the icy pavement.

"Happy!" I reached for the terrier, her light-colored coat now a mass of dirty fur. "Here, girl. We gotta get you home."

I held out a dog biscuit, and she came eagerly to take it. "Life on the street isn't so glamorous after all, huh?" I asked.

As I snapped a leash on Happy's collar I thought, *There's a reason for everything. Maybe this means that Caroline will forgive you.* But I knew I was kidding myself. It would take a lot more than finding a lost dog to earn Caroline's trust again.

Happy started tugging hard at the leash as soon as her house came into view. Handling two dogs and a bike was no simple task; it had taken nearly an hour to get to Mr. Francisco's place to return Red and another half hour to get to the Willises'. When we reached the door, she jumped up against the polished wood.

Someone must have heard her; I heard a quick rush of steps inside before I even rang the bell.

Caroline opened the door. She didn't even notice me at first—she was looking down.

"Oh, Happy, I thought I'd never see you again!" She dropped to her knees and hugged the dirty, wiggling dog. Happy tried to lick Caroline's face, and her tail wagged so furiously that her whole body shook.

"Oh, you're so cold, and your poor paws—I can't believe you're back in one piece."

Caroline looked up, as if realizing for the first time that someone held the end of the leash. "Jake!" She looked almost alarmed.

"Uh, hi," I said hesitantly. "I saw the sign about your dog, so I—"

"Mom!" Caroline called over her shoulder. "Happy's home!"

Mrs. Willis came down to the entryway and bent to pet the little dog, who still wiggled with joy. "What a relief," she said. "With the temperature dropping, I was afraid—" She didn't finish the sentence, but she looked up at me and smiled. "Hello again, Jake. Thank you so much for bringing Happy back. Hold on, let me get my purse—"

"Oh, no," I said. "I couldn't take the reward. Thanks anyhow. Caroline's a, um—"

Caroline looked up at me questioningly; when I met her eyes, she quickly turned back to the dog.

"A good friend," I finished. "That's why I did it."

Caroline kept petting the dog, whispering to her soothingly.

"If you're sure," Mrs. Willis said. She watched Caroline and Happy thoughtfully. "Thanks so much, Jake. You don't know how much this means to us." Mrs. Willis bent down again to rub the dog's head as I unclipped the leash and stuffed it back into my pocket.

"Let's go get you something to eat, girl," Mrs. Willis said as the dog followed her upstairs from the entryway.

Caroline stood up and brushed the little clumps of snow that had fallen from Happy's paws on her jeans.

"Caroline," I began, unsure of what to say. "I—"

"Thank you, Jake," she interrupted me quietly. "You didn't need to do that."

I glanced through the window in the Willises' front door. An icy sheen covered the street. "Not a good night to be out," I admitted sheepishly. "I'm just glad I found her. Can't believe I did, actually."

Caroline met my gaze, and as I took in the gleaming hazel of her eyes and the thickness of her lashes I recalled all the times I told Sid I wasn't aware of Caroline's looks. *But I did know she was gorgeous,* I realized silently. *I just wouldn't let myself face it.*

Here with Caroline now, it all came back to me. The way her lower lip curved in harmony with the arch of her brow. How the top of her head just reached the tip of my nose, and if I held her—*if* I held her, we would fit together perfectly. How right she'd feel in my arms. And as for kissing that curved lower lip, kissing both lips—

151

"You really outdid yourself, didn't you?" she asked, breaking the silence.

Something made me add, "But I—I did it for you, Caroline."

She took a step closer to me, and I almost reached out to touch her, to pull her into my arms. But I stopped abruptly when Caroline froze.

"How's everything going with Miranda?" she asked, turning to gaze blankly out the frost-covered window.

Miranda. Miranda suddenly seemed so far away, so far in the past.

I longed to tell Caroline I was sorry for everything I did. I needed so desperately to hold Caroline, to kiss her, to make everything right. But her one question cut straight to my heart.

"Caroline, I—"

The look she gave me then told me everything. She wasn't willing to forgive me—she had Wade Hamilton now. I was wrong to think any different.

Her tone went from cold to formal. "Thanks again for finding my dog, Jake. I have to go help my mom now." She sounded as if she were speaking to a total stranger, someone she never knew.

Maybe, to her, that's what I had become.

I wanted to say something more, but I couldn't. All I could do was open the door and walk outside. The night had never felt so cold. When I heard the door shut behind me, I shivered.

152

Big snowflakes drifted down from the dark sky, swirling in the glow of the porch lights, leaping up when the wind gusted. It should have been a beautiful scene, but it wasn't. It looked incredibly lonely.

I had made a terrible mistake.

FOURTEEN

THE SNOW CONTINUED to fall as I pedaled slowly, unsteadily home. I tried to warm up by imagining myself holding Caroline by a raging fireplace, the two of us watching the snow building up outside. Instead I was alone, chugging through the icy wind.

When I messed up, I really did it big time.

By the time I rolled my bike into our garage, my fingers and toes were numb, as well as my nose and cheeks. When I went into the kitchen, the rush of warm air felt good on my cold face. I pulled off my coat, hat, and gloves and washed my hands. The water made them tingle, but gradually the warmth returned.

The kitchen was empty, the counters clean. Dinner was long over. I looked in the fridge and found the full plate of steak and vegetables my mom had prepared for me. I stuck it in the microwave and poured myself a glass of milk.

I didn't realize just how hungry I was. But even after I cleared my plate, a troubling emptiness remained inside me.

All I could think about was Caroline. How could I have been so stupid? The frustration welled up from deep within me. I wanted to bang my head against the wall and shout, but a pain in my hand cut me short. I had been holding my fork so tightly that my knuckles were white and my fingers were cramped. I relaxed my hand and the fork dropped to the table with a clang.

I'd had my chance with Caroline, and I'd let it slip away—no, threw it away—because I was too thickheaded to see what was right in front of me. Now I knew all too painfully well, but there was no way to turn back time. Caroline was with Wade, and I was with Miranda. For better or for worse.

"I see you're back." My dad's voice cut through my gloom, making me jump a little. He shuffled over to the freezer and took out a frozen yogurt bar. "Did you find the missing dog?" he asked as he stripped off the paper wrapper.

I nodded. "Dogs, actually. I got them both home okay. Dad," I said, "can I ask you a question?"

"Sure." He pulled out a chair and sat down across the table from me, taking a bite of frozen yogurt.

"Suppose," I started slowly, "suppose a guy

thought he had this idea of what his dream girl would be. He thought he'd know her when he found her. When someone came along who fit all his requirements and was really pretty and sweet on top of it, he was sure he'd found the perfect girl."

"Sounds good so far," my dad commented. "And?"

"But what if after he went out with this girl for a while and he'd already asked her to a dance, a big dance, he realized that he—he actually liked another girl more?" I finished with a rush. I bit my lip and waited for my dad to answer.

He blinked behind his glasses and didn't respond for a moment. "What do *you* think this hypothetical guy should do, Jake?"

"I guess he's stuck, at least until after the dance," I said, poking my fork at my plate. "I mean, if he's already asked the girl, and she's bought an expensive dress and probably told all her friends that she's going—well, I guess he *has* to take her, even if he doesn't really want to anymore."

My dad smiled. "I think you're right," he said. "There's such a thing as gentlemanly behavior, or just plain keeping a promise."

I nodded. It sounded like the right thing to do, but it didn't make me feel much better.

"One more thing," I started, then hesitated. This was even harder to explain, but my dad waited patiently until I got my words straight. "What if this new girl—what if he's made her mad? Maybe he put her down without meaning to and really hurt her feelings. Do you think she'd ever give him another chance?"

"I'd say the guy should wait a while," my dad said. "She'd have time to get over her anger, and he could break things off with the other girl. Then I think he should apologize to the girl he really likes, maybe call her or send her a note telling her how much he'd like to see her again. You just have to take your chances, Jake. Or this other guy would, I mean."

I laughed reluctantly. "I guess you know who the guy is," I told him.

"I guess so," my dad said. "Hang in there, Jake. Did I ever tell you about the time in college when I called to ask your mom's roommate out, but she thought the message was for her? When I showed up at the pizza place, two very angry girls were waiting for me."

"You didn't," I said, trying to imagine my parents as college students.

"Fortunately they decided it was funny instead of just awful, and the three of us ate an enormous amount of pizza and laughed a lot. That night I discovered that I liked your mother more than I liked her roommate. So after that I always made sure I called the right girl."

"Who's talking about me?" my mother said, looking into the kitchen. She came over and put her arms around my dad, leaning against him. "Telling all our secrets, are you?"

"Not quite all," my dad said, grinning up at her.

I looked at them and thought how I'd like to be like that in a few years, with someone to hug me and love me even if I made dumb mistakes. In my mind's eye that someone somehow looked a lot like Caroline.

But for now I was stuck with the golden girl. And I couldn't believe how bad that made me feel.

The light from Sid's bedroom window shone through the bare branches of the trees between our houses, creating a fractured pattern across my desk. I was trying to finish my homework, but it was too hard to concentrate. Staring out my window, I remembered how Sid and I used flashlights to send secret messages to each other when we were little kids. Now we weren't even talking to each other.

I picked up the phone and dialed his number. "Mrs. Halleman? It's Jake. Could I speak to Sid, please?"

My eyes were drawn to a shadow of movement on Sid's bedroom wall. "Yo," I heard him say over the line.

"Hey, Sid," I responded. "Could you come over for a minute?"

"Don't know; I've got a report to finish." His tone was chilly.

"This won't take long," I said. "But it's important. I really need to talk to you."

"Major conference time, huh? Okay, I'll be there in five."

His shadow moved around the room, then disappeared. I went downstairs and opened the front door before he even had a chance to knock.

"Thanks for coming over," I said.

He nodded. "It's cool."

Kristen walked by just then with a box of cookies. "Hi, Sid," she mumbled as she chewed.

"Hi," he replied quietly.

"Come on upstairs," I said, not wanting my little sister to hear any of our conversation.

Sid followed me. We went into my room, and I checked the hallway before closing the door.

"What's up?" he asked, dropping into my desk chair. "You're acting as if the CIA is after you."

"Little sisters make better spies," I said dryly, wondering how to start. "Listen, Sid, I'm sorry I jumped on you for what you said about Miranda the other night."

"In that case, I won't call you a moron again," Sid said. "At least not for a day or two." He dropped his arms and sat down in my desk chair, looking a little more relaxed. "You know, I couldn't believe it when Miranda broke up with you before, Jake. At the time you guys seemed good together. But come on, I mean, I know she's blond and gorgeous and has got a great body and all, but you've

160

gotta face it. She's not the girl of your dreams."

"I know, Sid. I've already faced it, and I don't know why it took me so long. I wish I was as lucky as you are," I told him.

Sid nodded. "Yeah, Shelley's pretty great. I've invited her over for Hanukkah dinner with my family. And we're going to the Winter Formal too."

"That's cool. But I thought we were going to double," I said.

"Well, since Miranda dumped—uh, you and Miranda broke up, I just figured . . ." Sid trailed off. "Anyhow, Shelley and Miranda aren't the best of friends. The blond goddess probably has her own ideas about who to hang around with at the dance."

"Actually, I think she does," I admitted.

"Hey, we can still hang out," Sid pointed out.

I nodded. "No problem. I just wish I had figured it out earlier, like you did," I said slowly.

"Figured out what?"

"That just because Miranda is blond and gorgeous doesn't mean I should fall in love with her. It doesn't really work, the two of us."

"I tried to tell you that, but you wouldn't listen," Sid reminded. "So, you got everything straight now?"

"Hardly. You're going to the dance with the girl you like," I grumbled. "Me, I'm still stuck with—"

"The blond barracuda," Sid finished for me.

"*Miranda,*" I said dryly. "And now that my matchmaking plans for Caroline seem to have worked, I don't think she'll give me another chance."

FIFTEEN

FRIDAY WAS A restless, uncomfortable day. It was the last day before our holiday break, and no one wanted to work, not even—it seemed to me—the teachers. All I wanted to do was run and hide. I didn't want to face either Miranda or Caroline.

At lunch I vowed to stay at my table with Sid. I waved at Miranda a couple of times but didn't want to go over and talk. I had to help her that afternoon with the decorations, and I wasn't looking forward to it.

As for Caroline, I tried not to even look in her direction. What she thought of me, I hated to guess.

"What the heck are you doing?" Sid demanded when I slid farther down in my seat.

"I don't want to see Miranda again today. I

163

don't want to sit with her, and I don't want to talk to her. I can't tell her how crazy about her I am when I'm not."

I brought some burned french fries up to my mouth, then I put them down. "All she can talk about is the dance. I'm dreading the dance."

"Rough." Sid took a big bite of his hamburger. "Pass the ketchup."

"And I really want to see Caroline, but there's no point because she won't let me tell her how I feel. She hates me, Sid. And now I have to keep officially dating Miranda—"

"Hold up, Jake. Miranda alert at three o'clock," Sid murmured.

Miranda came buzzing over to my right side, beaming like she was the happiest girl in the world. "Hi, honey," she said, bending down and kissing me on the cheek. "Can't wait till tomorrow night," she whispered in my ear as she rubbed my shoulders seductively. She didn't even wait for a response before taking off again.

I sighed. "See what I mean? I have to keep this up until we get this stupid dance behind us. Then I can break up with her. I just have to hope I don't make her as depressed as she made me. I'm a horrible person," I said gloomily.

"Horrible," Sid agreed. "Can I have your fries if you're not going to eat them?"

When I pushed my tray over, I thought briefly that fasting was just what I should be doing to

164

punish myself. Hadn't I read in history class about medieval monks fasting and wearing robes of horsehair?

While I was contemplating old-fashioned forms of penitence, Sid added, "I don't want to burst your bubble, but I don't think Miranda has even noticed you're trying to avoid her. She doesn't seem to notice *you* at all."

I groaned. "I know; she's busy with the decorating committee. That's all she can talk about, that and the dance itself. She's going to hate me forever."

"So?" Sid dipped a french fry into his ketchup.

I glared at him and stood up. Just then I caught a glimpse of Caroline. She was deep in conversation with Wade, and she looked better than ever.

Too bad, Magee, I had to tell myself. *She's too far gone now. Totally unobtainable—and it's all your fault.* I shuddered, feeling the gravity of my mistake.

"I'm going to the library to study till the bell rings," I told Sid. "You can have all my lunch."

"Hey, I should make sure you stay messed up a little longer," Sid replied, grinning as he dug into the cold, burned fries.

"Can you bring that pile of snowflakes over here, please? No, *that* one," Miranda demanded.

The hotel ballroom was a mess. I cursed myself for agreeing to help with the Winter Formal decorations. Despite the number of girls there, the work was slow going. I was the only guy around. But I couldn't back out on Miranda now.

The girls rushed around the ballroom, over-flowing with enthusiasm about the dance. I grabbed an enormous stack of large white card-board snowflakes and a ladder and sulked over to where Miranda had been standing. Meanwhile she and Kara discussed where to hang the sliver foil icicles.

While I taped up the snowflakes, a thought sud-denly occurred to me. The angel gifts! I felt a rush of cold go through my entire body. How could I forget that so easily? I had bought all those gifts for six-year-old Kevin, and I even wrapped them my-self. And tonight was the last night they could be dropped off at the volunteer table in the mall.

I'd been so wrapped up in my own problems, I'd forgotten something much more important. How could I have been so stupid?

The clock on the wall read 4:30. Just enough time to get home, grab the presents, and take them to the mall. But I had to finish this job first.

I climbed down from the ladder and grabbed a pile of icicles. Then I found an undecorated ledge and started hanging them there.

"Wait, sweetie, we haven't decided where to put them yet," Miranda complained.

"This will work," I told her. "Trust me."

She frowned, but after I put up a few more, she

nodded. "That *does* look pretty good. Okay, Kara, we'll put them on this side."

I groaned quietly and kept my eye on the clock. I thought I had messed up enough already. Now if I didn't get my angel gifts in on time, Christmas would be ruined completely.

With only a week to go till Christmas, the mall was completely overcrowded with last-minute shoppers. The mad rush for gifts reminded me that I hadn't bought Miranda a present. It was funny— after all my grumbling about being alone for the holidays, I was preparing to break up with Miranda as soon as I could. Should I buy her a gift to ease the blow? What if she'd already bought me something? I'd feel awful with nothing to offer in return.

I passed by the shop where Miranda was going to buy the blue party dress. There was still plenty of time to spare before the mall closed; maybe they sold stuff to go with the dress. After hanging around the door for a minute or two, I finally got the nerve to go inside.

"May I help you?" a motherly-looking salesperson asked.

"I, uh, I wondered—about that blue dress in the window. The girl I'm taking to the dance—I think she bought one the other day," I stammered. Was I making any sense? "I was wondering, uh, do you have anything to go with it that I might get her as, you know, a gift?"

"An accessory? What a thoughtful idea. Let's see what we can find." She brought out a hair clip covered with blue beads.

"That's nice," I said. "I hope she didn't buy one already. Do you remember her? Pretty, with long blond hair and blue eyes? I think she and her mother bought the dress last night."

"I didn't sell a dress like that this whole week," the salesperson said. "Clara, did you sell the blue waltz-length to a young lady with blond hair?"

The woman named Clara wrinkled her nose as she rang up a sale. "I sold one two weeks ago to a pretty blond; she bought everything we had that matched the dress too, as I remember."

I frowned. That couldn't have been Miranda, but still . . . "Maybe I'll come back later," I told them. "Thanks for your help."

Miranda couldn't have bought the dress before I asked her to the dance last night, I thought as I ran to the center court of the mall. Not unless she bought it when we were first dating. No—she *did* tell me last night that she would be coming back to buy the dress. The salesperson must have been confused.

The volunteer table came into view, and I forgot everything else. Caroline sat behind it, wearing a red sweatshirt with a Christmas tree design on the front. I ran over and put my bag on the table before she could help anyone else.

"Hi, Caroline," I said breathlessly. "I brought

the gifts for my angel. His name and number are on the labels."

"Thanks for bringing your presents in," Caroline said without smiling at me.

As she looked in the shopping bag she made some notes on her clipboard and stacked the gifts with the others that had been piled all around the table. She didn't look up at me.

"Do you need any help tomorrow with delivering them?" I asked. "I'd be glad to pitch in."

"We have a volunteer who'll help us with that," she said coolly. "Thanks anyway, Jake."

"Anyone I know?" I asked. Was it Wade? I tried not to think of another guy working side by side with Caroline, brushing her arm, standing a little too close . . .

Had Wade kissed her yet?

Caroline grinned, seemingly amused by my concern. I was relieved to see her smile, even though it was at my expense. "It's no one you know," she said, as if she read my thoughts. "He's a retiree, one of the part-time workers at the thrift store."

"Oh," I replied, feeling like an idiot.

The volunteer table was busy, and I had to move out of the way for a couple with their arms full of packages.

"So, Jake, are you taking Miranda to the formal?" she asked warily. She looked directly into my eyes, almost daring me to answer.

"Yeah, actually," I answered, shifting uncomfortably. "Are you and—"

"Excuse me, please," an obnoxious male voice came from behind me. "Can you move it along? Some of us have business to take care of here."

"I—I'll see you around, Jake," Caroline said, motioning for the person to step forward.

"I thought you two lovebirds would never shut up," the man said, dropping his gifts on the table as I turned away.

But not before Caroline gave me the most heartbreaking look I had ever seen.

Blinking, I detoured past the decorated tree, the giant candy canes, and the elves' village. All around, lights twinkled and red bows adorned every storefront. Little kids still waited in line to see Santa, and couples walked hand in hand.

All around, people were happy. I should have been happy too. After all, I was going to the dance with a beautiful girl, the girl I'd dreamed about for so long.

The only problem was, she wasn't Caroline.

SIXTEEN

"WHY AREN'T YOU more excited?" my sister asked sarcastically on Saturday morning. "Isn't tonight the big dance?"

I nodded, walking into the kitchen to get some cereal. Kristen followed me.

"Don't split your face or anything," Kristen said, taking a glass from the cupboard and reaching for the milk. "I'd be excited. I can't wait till I'm old enough to go to a dance."

I shrugged. If I were picking up Caroline tonight instead of Miranda, I would be a lot more excited. But as it was—

"I'd have a new dress, and I'd spend all day on my hair," Kristen said dreamily, sipping her milk. She added, glancing at me, "And hopefully my date will be as cute as you are."

I smiled in spite of myself. For a little sister, she

171

wasn't so bad. "In three years I'm sure the guys will be beating down the door," I told her.

"Jake, it's for you!" Kristen called from downstairs.

I picked up the receiver in the hall outside my bedroom. "'Lo."

"Jake, it's Sid. I'm going over to the mall to pick up my tux and the corsage. You coming?"

"Okay," I said, grabbing my jacket and heading down the stairs. When I got to Sid's driveway, he and his dad were standing beside the car.

"Tonight's the big night, eh, Jake?" Mr. Halleman said.

I smiled as politely as I could. "Yes, sir."

As we got in the car Sid twisted around to look at me. "Try to restrain your enthusiasm," he said dryly.

When we got to the formal shop, the woman behind the counter brought out two plastic-sheathed hangers. "You can try them on in there to make sure the fit is correct," she said, nodding toward the rooms in the back.

"Looks okay to me," I said.

She looked at me strangely, and Sid elbowed me in the side.

"Come on, snap out of it," he hissed. "Try on the tux and stop acting like you're going to your own funeral."

I dragged myself into a small booth, pulled off

my jeans and sweater, and slipped into and out of the tux as quickly as possible.

"It's fine," I told the woman when I came out.

Sid took a lot longer. When he was finally finished, we headed over to the florist. I'd had specific instructions from Miranda to order a white-and-blue carnation combination on a wristband. The florist gave it to me to inspect, but I barely looked at it.

"Nice," I said emotionlessly, paying the bill.

"Your young lady will be very pleased, I'm sure," he said.

"Hope so," I replied.

On the way home Sid said, "I'm taking Shelley to the Blue Hen for dinner."

"Nice place," I responded. "You guys will have fun."

"Where are you taking Miranda?" Sid eyed me curiously.

"I'm not."

Sid scowled. "Jake, come on, you have to—"

"No, you don't understand," I interrupted. "We're going to a predance party at Kara Robbins's house. Miranda's whole crowd is going to be there. It's what she wanted to do."

"Jeez," Sid said. "I thought dropping a lot of money on an expensive dinner was hard. But I'd rather do that than hang out with a lot of people I didn't really like."

"Tell me about it," I growled.

*   *   *

I took the tux out of the garment bag with the same sort of excitement I'd feel getting a death sentence. Where had all my enthusiasm for dating Miranda gone? I had dreamed for months of taking Miranda to a formal dance, and now the big night was just a couple of hours away. But Caroline's face always came into my mind when I tried to picture Miranda in that amazing pale blue gown.

When I got out of the shower, I towel-dried my hair and opened a new bottle of aftershave. Would Caroline like this scent—

Miranda, I reminded myself hastily. I meant Miranda. I had to stay focused on Miranda.

I dressed slowly, struggling with the cummerbund and bow tie, and finally got everything in the right place. When I slipped into the black jacket and looked at myself in the mirror, a stranger looked back at me.

Not bad, I thought, looking at my reflection. Pretty cool, in fact. James Bond, look out. Caroline would be impressed. . . .

Miranda, you dolt, I reminded myself. *Miranda is your date tonight. And you're going to be late if you don't get moving.* I dragged myself downstairs and took the boxed corsage from the refrigerator.

"I'm leaving," I called.

"Let's see, Jake," my mother said, running out to meet me. "Don't you look nice! Here, come stand in the living room so I can take your picture."

"Oh, Mom," I groaned. "Make it quick, okay? I don't want to be late." The truth was, I did, but what would she think if I told her that?

After she snapped a bunch of pictures, Mom kissed me on the cheek. "Have a good time, sweetheart," she said.

Kristen beamed at me. "You have to tell me all about it when you get home, Jake," she said.

All this encouragement from my mom and sister made me feel good—and sad at the same time. While they meant well, they had no idea that the dance couldn't be wonderful without Caroline.

My dad nodded and clapped me on the back. "You'll be fine, Jake," he said quietly, leaning in close so that no one else could hear. "Once the dance starts, I'm sure you'll have a great time."

After a heated discussion over whether or not I should wear my parka over my tux (I lost), I reluctantly headed out to the car wrapped in Dad's wool overcoat.

The sky was fading rapidly to darkness. The streets were clear enough, with a little slush at the sides. The snow on the lawns glittered with a topping of ice crystals. Christmas lights shone from houses here and there, and the air was very clear and sharp. It was a beautiful winter night, a perfect night for a romantic formal dance. But it would never be truly perfect—not without Caroline.

My breath clouded the frosty air as I walked up the sidewalk to Miranda's house. On our last date

I'd been overcome with anxiety after I rang her bell. But tonight I was totally calm. With my old feelings for Miranda fading, I was losing my old nervousness too.

"Hello, Jake," Mrs. Thomas said when she answered the door. "Come in. Miranda will be right down."

"Thanks," I said casually as I walked inside and wiped my feet on the mat. A rustle of movement stopped me in my tracks.

Miranda stood poised at the top of the stairs, then came down slowly, moving gracefully in her full skirt. The dress—pale as icicles—floated around her, and her blue eyes were wide with excitement. Her blond hair had been pulled into a sort of twist that was held with a clip that looked a lot like the one I'd almost bought her. Sparkling diamonds decorated her earlobes.

I was momentarily knocked breathless. "You look beautiful," I said honestly. "Like a movie star."

Miranda beamed back at me. "You look nice too, Jake," she said.

We stood in the hallway and posed for what seemed like a whole roll of film. When her mom was finally finished, Miranda went to get her coat. She came back wrapped up to her neck in rolls of fur.

"You're wearing a fur coat?" I blurted.

She flushed. Sounding defensive, she said, "It's my grandmother's coat—it's mink. She lent it to me for tonight. I wouldn't buy a fur coat myself, of course, but she offered, so—"

I thought of the dogs and cats that I groomed at the kennels—the smooth touch of their coats and the trust in their dark eyes when they looked at me as I brushed them gently. They were alive and they had feelings. I looked at the thick mink pelts in the coat and repressed a shiver. I thought of a hundred things to say, but I swallowed hard and pushed them back. This was not the time to argue about fur coats.

We went outside into the cold air and walked up the sidewalk. The party was only three houses away. Miranda tucked her hand into my arm so she wouldn't slip on the ice.

"I can't believe tonight is finally here. I've waited so long for this dance."

I felt a twinge of guilt; Miranda seemed so happy to be going to the dance with me, and here I was just waiting for a chance to break up with her. Would I end up breaking her heart as badly as she had broken mine? Would she think I was just doing it for revenge? I felt pretty terrible about the whole thing. But the idea of staying with her when I felt the way I did about Caroline made me feel even worse. Yet who was to say if I took the step and broke up with Miranda for Caroline that she'd forgive me?

When I realized that Miranda was talking, I struggled to pull my thoughts back and pay attention. "What?"

177

"I said, we're here," she repeated. "Come on, my feet are cold." She hurried up the walkway and rang the bell as I followed. Kara opened the door immediately.

"There you are," Kara said. "Come on in."

Miranda introduced me around. I already knew most of the girls from Miranda's decorating committee, and I recognized a lot of their dates, though there were a couple of guys from St. Andrew's. The food that had been laid out in the dining room held a bit more interest for me. After Miranda and I filled our plates, we sat down on the couch to eat.

The girls laughed and talked while the guys just sat and ate. It was pretty obvious to see which group was more excited about the dance. Fortunately Miranda didn't seem to mind—or even notice— that I was not being the life of the party.

Kara and her date, Chad, were sitting on the sofa beside us. When Miranda got up to get a mineral water, Chad winked at me.

"Having fun, Jake?"

"Sure," I said, still determined to be polite.

"Yeah, she's a gorgeous girl," he agreed. Kara frowned at him, and he added, "Me, I like red-heads, of course."

"Right." I ate the last of my roast beef and stood up to take my plate back to the table.

"Miranda's a super girl, all right," Chad added. "Better enjoy it while you can." He smirked.

Kara kicked him.

"Ouch," Chad said. "Hey, Kara, I didn't—"

Just when I set my plate down, I heard Mrs. Robbins ask, "Is everyone ready to go?"

"Oh, I need to check my makeup, Mom," Kara said.

"I should make sure my hair isn't coming down," Miranda added.

Kara, Miranda, and the rest of the girls went off in a flurry to Kara's bedroom, leaving us guys to stand around and talk about the last boys' basketball game. A few of the guys asked me my opinion on some of the key plays, but all it did was remind me of Caroline. I answered them absently as I stared out the window and wondered if Caroline was handing out the angel tree gifts now.

When the girls came back, I helped Miranda into her tacky coat. Then everyone loaded into the Robbinses' family van. The girls had already planned on riding over together, but they hadn't planned on how cramped we would all be in one vehicle. So now the girls announced that everyone not wearing a dress had to cram in the back, leaving enough room so that all the big, billowy formals wouldn't get messed up.

Miranda ended up in the front passenger seat, and I was secretly relieved that we were too far apart to talk.

At the hotel I helped Miranda out of the van, and we walked as a group toward the hotel entrance. All I could think about was how excited I would have been to be here with Miranda a month ago and how ecstatic I would be to have Caroline on my arm now.

Music blared from inside. Just ahead of us a beautiful girl in a long red gown was gliding in, her date holding the door open for her.

"Whoa, check it out," a guy's voice came from behind me, quickly followed by the sound of a purse smacking against a beefy shoulder.

The beautiful girl was Caroline. And Wade was her date.

SEVENTEEN

"WHAT'S WRONG, JAKE?" Miranda asked, grabbing my arm. "Did you slip on some ice or something?"

I shook my head no, cursing myself. I must have jerked when I saw Caroline and Wade. Gritting my teeth, I took a deep breath. *So, smart guy,* I thought, *you should have been prepared for this. Don't let everyone notice that you're thinking about someone else's girl. Tonight is Miranda's night. Think about her feelings, you dope.*

Miranda was staring at me, concern on her face.

"Sorry, Miranda," I said quickly.

"Do you have the tickets?" she asked impatiently.

I suddenly realized that we were at the door and everyone behind us was waiting to go in.

"It's cold out here, man," Chad complained. "Get a move on."

"Oh, yeah. Right." Once I handed over the tickets, Miranda and I were waved toward the ballroom.

I took a deep breath once we walked inside. The ballroom looked great. The icicles and snowflakes glittered in the lights. A band played from a raised platform at the front of the floor, and already couples were dancing. It looked like someone's romantic dream come true, but unfortunately it wasn't mine.

In the back of my mind I had figured that Caroline would be helping with the angel tree gifts tonight. I didn't expect to see her here. She and Wade must really be serious after all.

Thanks to me, Caroline had found her perfect guy.

Thanks to me, it wasn't me.

"Jake, are you feeling all right?" Miranda asked.

"Sure," I lied. I had to get ahold of myself fast. Using the coat check as an excuse, I walked away and tried to clear my head. But I couldn't stop looking over at Caroline. The coat checker actually had to wave the claim slips in front of my face to snap me out of it.

When I got back to the table, I found another excuse to get away. "Want some punch?" I asked Miranda.

After she nodded, I walked across the dance floor to the long table laden with punch and desserts, hoping to get a closer look at Caroline and Wade.

Caroline looked incredible. Her long dark hair was pulled back from her face, hanging free down her back in a stream of curls that just brushed her smooth skin. Her lips were touched with color, and a delicate gold strand encircled her neck. She wore a deep red dress that made her eyes look even brighter than usual, and her whole face seemed to glow.

Unfortunately Wade was putting the rest of us guys to shame. He wore a tux with as much ease as he had worn the clown costume. Looking at him made me feel like an impostor, like a little kid dressing up.

And the way Caroline smiled at him—that didn't make me feel good at all. Could she be that serious about him already?

As I watched, Wade reached out and put one arm around Caroline's shoulders. I clenched my fists, wanting to push him away from her.

Not that I would, of course, but a guy could dream.

As Caroline lifted a glass of punch to her lips I remembered that I was supposed to be getting some myself. But when I got back to the table, a cup in each hand, Miranda wasn't there.

"Where'd Miranda go?" I asked Kara, the only person at the table. She frowned and nodded toward the dance floor.

Miranda was dancing with Chad.

"You could be a little more attentive," Kara

snapped. "Chad's starting to feel sorry for Miranda, you know."

I suspected that Chad was feeling a lot more than that. He was finding every opportunity to make a move. Poor Kara. Chad was blatantly ignoring her. But then I realized that I was doing practically the same thing to Miranda.

"Want to dance?" I asked Kara lamely.

Kara nodded, and we went out and finished the dance together in silence. When it ended, I led her over to Miranda and Chad, and we switched partners.

This tune was a slower one than the last—slow and achingly romantic. I put my arms around Miranda, and we began to sway. Once this had been my dream; now all I wanted to do was to turn around and look at Caroline again.

"Ouch," Miranda said. "You stepped on my foot, Jake. What's wrong with you tonight?"

"Sorry," I muttered. "My mistake."

Was it ever. *If you'd had your head on straight, Magee,* I told myself grimly, *you could have been here tonight with Caroline. Now you get to watch her with another guy.*

It was going to be a very long evening.

As if to prove my point, I saw Caroline and Wade go out on the floor. They rocked gently to the music, and it seemed to me that he was holding her much too tight.

"I didn't think Wade was so pushy," I muttered.

Miranda looked at me. "What do you care?" she asked. I could hear suspicion in her voice.

I remembered what my father told me: I had an obligation to my date. As I recalled what he had said about promises and gentlemanly behavior, I swallowed hard. "I don't," I finally replied guiltily.

Miranda suddenly stopped dancing. "Come on, Jake. Let's get our pictures taken before my hair comes down," she said.

I followed her to the photographer's area with the same anticipation I reserved for taking out the garbage. Miranda checked her makeup in a tiny mirror while we stood in line, waiting for our turn.

"Have you voted for the Snow Queen yet?" Miranda asked after the photographer took his last shot.

I shook my head no, and she grimaced. "Go and vote right now," she demanded. "The voting box is over by the door."

"Aren't you coming?"

"I already voted while you were hanging around the punch table," she said briskly. "But you have to vote too."

It was pretty obvious who she expected me to vote for. I dragged myself to the voting box, picked up a ballot, and voted for Miranda. I didn't really know the other girls listed anyhow. When I saw Sid approaching, looking cool in his dark tux, I put my ballot in the box.

"How's it going?" Sid asked. "You look about as cheerful as my dad does when Michigan loses."

"Caroline's here," I said.

"That's bad?" He glanced around.

"With Wade," I pointed out.

"Oh," he said. "That *is* bad."

"Where's Shelley?" I asked him.

"In the bathroom, getting ready for our photos. You done that already?"

I nodded glumly. "*A precious memento of a memorable night.* That's what the sign said."

Sid laughed. "Hey, tonight won't last forever," he said.

"Tell me that again in an hour." I took a deep breath. "Guess I better get back."

"See you later," Sid said. "Cheer up, okay?"

"Right." I headed back for our table, and again Kara was the only one there.

"I really wish you'd stay with your date," she snarled.

"Miranda wanted me to go vote," I snapped back. "Maybe *you* should talk to *Chad*."

She scowled, and I turned to look for Caroline. She was sitting down at one of the tables, talking to Wade. She seemed perfectly happy.

I'd blown my chance with her completely. Caroline was lost to me forever.

With no hope left for me at all, I figured I might as well try to make Miranda happy.

When the music ended, I reclaimed Miranda

186

from Chad, and we danced to the next song. "Please don't hold me so tight," Miranda said. "I don't want to crush my dress. And watch out, don't touch my hair."

"We already had our pictures taken," I pointed out.

"There might be more later," she said, not quite meeting my eyes.

Oh, yeah, if she won the vote for Snow Queen. I held her carefully while we danced to the slow music, not connecting at all. As my mind wandered, the vision of Caroline came to me: Caroline in my arms, drifting to the music, laying her head against my cheek without caring about messing up her hair, Caroline smiling at me, those glossy, red lips parting . . .

"The music stopped, Jake," Miranda said, jolting me back to reality. "Let's see who's around."

Miranda flitted around the tables like a regular social butterfly, but I couldn't keep up with her. As I headed back to the table I heard her urge, "Now don't forget to vote," for what seemed like the thousandth time.

"Do you think Miranda'll win?" I asked Kara when I sat down.

Kara looked at me like I was crazy. "Have you had your head in the sand, Jake? Do you have any idea how hard Miranda has worked on this dance? Of course she's going to win. She's done more than anyone to make this dance a success."

"Oh," I said weakly. "Good for her."

Miranda was still fluttering around, so I decided to go look for Sid and Shelley. When I got out to the hallway, I saw something that made me feel as though I had been punched in the stomach.

Caroline was out there, alone, standing by the pay phone, one hand to her face.

She was crying.

EIGHTEEN

W HAT HAD WADE done to make Caroline cry? I wanted to hunt him down and push his face into the punch bowl. But I knew that it would be better for me to stay with Caroline and find out what was wrong.

The sight of Caroline crying was devastating. I felt something twist inside me. I reached out to touch her, then remembered, with an almost physical pain, that I didn't have the right to do that.

"Caroline," I asked quietly, "what's wrong?"

"They've lost the gifts," she said, sobbing again. "The Christmas gifts for the children."

I blinked, trying to digest her words. "How could anyone lose a truckload of presents?"

"That's just it. They've lost the truck." She took a deep breath, visibly trying to control herself. "They were supposed to be giving out the gifts, like

189

right now, any minute. All the kids are at the community center, and they have someone dressed up as Santa—I called my mom there to see how it was going, and she told me—"

"How, Caroline?" I asked slowly, thinking of Kevin and all those other kids waiting for the gifts that might never come. No Christmas for any of those kids? The idea tore me apart. "How could that happen?"

"There were two men in the truck." Caroline wiped her eyes, trying to calm down. "The truck broke down, and one of the men went for help. But he's sort of old, and he started having chest pains. A delivery truck driver picked him up a few streets away and took him to a hospital. He'd had a mild heart attack, and Mom says he'll be all right, but he's not able to tell anyone where the truck broke down. The man who brought him to the emergency room left before anyone thought to ask him."

"But what about the other man in the truck? Won't he do something if the first man doesn't come back?"

Caroline looked at me. "You don't understand. The other man, Stanley, he's—he's what my mom calls 'mentally challenged.'"

"Oh," I said. "So he won't know what to do, maybe?"

Caroline nodded. "He does well when he follows directions, but a new situation—if Mr. Powers told him to stay in the truck, that's what he'll do.

He'll stay in the truck all night, waiting for someone to come. And all the gifts will wait with him."

"Can't they do something?"

"Mom says several people are out looking, but they don't know what route the drivers were taking. So far, they haven't found the truck."

The truck will be found eventually, I thought, *but maybe not in time for the party.*

"How can I enjoy the dance, thinking about the kids waiting for their gifts?" Caroline said. She gulped back another sob.

"We're not," I said, decision in my voice. "We're going to do something. We're going to find that truck." No way was I letting Christmas pass by those kids.

Besides, I'd walk across the whole city myself if it would take that despondent look out of Caroline's eyes.

But walking wasn't really practical; we needed wheels. I groaned, suddenly remembering that I had left my car at Miranda's house. "We need a few kids with cars," I explained. "Who do you think might help?"

"I don't know." Caroline looked more hopeful as she seemed to realize what I was thinking. "Let's start asking."

Caroline headed for a group of girls, and I spotted Miranda talking to Danny Erickson and a few of his friends. I dashed over to them.

"We need some help," I told them.

"What's the matter?" Miranda lifted her brows. "Did someone get hurt?"

"Sort of." I explained quickly about the Christmas gifts, the missing truck, and our idea to go out and help search for them both.

"Poor kids," Danny said as the others nodded in agreement. "I'll help. I've got my pickup."

"A truck would be great," I said. "If we can find the broken-down truck, we could carry all the packages."

Miranda nodded. "That's a nice idea. As soon as the dance is over we'll—"

"No," I said. "You don't understand. Those kids are at the center *now*. We have to find the gifts as soon as possible."

"You can't leave yet!" Miranda's eyes widened, and her voice rose in near panic. "I worked so hard on this dance. And the voting—they'll crown the Snow Queen soon—and—and—"

"I already voted," I told her, trying to soothe her. "But I can't stay here and party when little kids are missing out on their Christmas."

"If you leave now, Jake Magee, I'll never speak to you again!" Miranda's voice shrilled.

"I'm sorry, Miranda, but I think this is more important. I voted for you, and I really do hope you're crowned queen. But I'm going. This is something I have to do. Do you understand?"

Miranda lifted her chin. "You're just doing it for her," she said, nodding toward Caroline. Had

Miranda actually taken notice of me and Caroline last week?

"No," I said. "I mean, that's part of it, but I would try to help the kids even if Caroline had nothing to do with it."

"Sure." Miranda turned and stalked off.

Danny went to get his coat, and his two friends agreed to go. Caroline came back with two more juniors. Wade wasn't one of them.

"What about Wade?" I asked.

"He's going to stay; he didn't seem too enthused about leaving the party," Caroline said. "But we have two trucks, one car, and five kids, plus you and me. Or at least me." She paused, a thoughtful look spreading over her face. "You don't have to go, Jake. Miranda looks pretty upset. And she's probably going to be crowned Snow Queen too. She'll want you to be with her."

"I already told Miranda I'm going," I said shortly. "I want those kids to get their presents. Miranda still has lots of friends here."

Caroline looked at me, her dark eyes serious. "Are you sure?"

"Absolutely," I said. "I just wish I had my car."

"Why don't you ride with Danny and me?" Caroline suggested. "I know some of the routes the volunteers might have taken. We'll meet at the parking lot entrance in five minutes and divide up the areas the truck might have gone so that we don't waste our efforts."

"Right," I said. "I'll get my coat." On the way back I ran into Wade.

"Hey, Wade," I said. "You're staying here, right?"

He nodded.

"Miranda's not real happy about my leaving," I told him. "If she's crowned queen, maybe you could escort her up to be crowned? I'm not trying to ruin her evening—I just think finding the toys for the kids is more important."

He stared at me, then nodded slowly. "No problem. She'll be in safe hands with me," he said. "Her boyfriend is actually my cousin—he goes to St. Andrew's. But since he broke his leg last week, he couldn't take her to the dance. It was nice of you to step in at the last minute."

"Uh-huh," I responded, letting it sink in. A few weeks ago—a few *days* ago—I would have been crushed. But tonight I just laughed.

I didn't need to worry anymore about Miranda; she could obviously take pretty good care of herself. "Thanks, Wade," I said as I turned toward the exit with only one thing on my mind.

Caroline and I had to rescue Christmas.

NINETEEN

"I GUESS WE'RE the best-dressed search party in town," Caroline said nervously as she sat in between me and Danny in the cab of Danny's truck. She and I were pressed together so closely, I became acutely aware of every breath she took, every movement of her body. My arm lay against her arm, and when she turned her head to scan the dark streets, her dark hair brushed my cheek. I caught a light scent, like flowers in spring, and it made me tingle all the way down to my toes.

It wasn't easy to focus my attention on the search, but Caroline's concern kept me in line. We cruised past islands of light reflected by streetlamps and stared hard at the dark stretches in between. There were plenty of cars and trucks parked at the sides of the streets, and every time we saw one that

Caroline thought was similar to the shelter truck, we had to slow and inspect it carefully.

But each time Caroline would shake her head and say, "That's not it," and we'd be off again. It was a slow process.

We drove for almost an hour, searching one dark street after another. More than once I caught a glint of tears in Caroline's eyes.

I wanted to reassure her and suggest that even if we didn't find the gifts tonight, we could track down the children and hand them out once they were found. But it wouldn't be the same on any other night. The broken Christmas promise would remain with the children for a long time. One more disappointment for kids who had likely known too many.

"I wanted them to have one happy Christmas," Caroline said softly. She must have been thinking the same thing.

I glanced at my watch. "They're still at the community center," I told her. "They'll stay for a while, right?"

Caroline nodded. "They have games for them, and cookies and punch. But if we don't get there with the gifts, Santa can't come. That's what they're all waiting for."

"We'll find the truck," I told her, reaching over and squeezing her hand. This time, unlike at the basketball game, she wasn't startled by it. She returned the pressure and sighed heavily.

After ten more minutes Danny pulled the truck over to the curb. "Well, we've covered our designated area," he said. "We'd just waste our time if we double-checked someone else's."

"We can't stop," Caroline protested. "The truck has to be somewhere!"

A stray cat wandered through an alley and slunk out of sight. I watched it, hoping it had somewhere warm to go tonight. Then a thought hit me.

"Caroline, do you think he might have taken a shortcut?" I asked. "Maybe cut through some of these back streets? We've only been covering the main drags."

She looked at me. "Why would Mr. Powers do that?"

"Who knows? He's lying in a hospital bed right now. By the time we're able to ask him, it will be too late for the Christmas party."

"Okay, Jake," Caroline said, still unsure. "It's worth a try. Anything's worth a try at this point."

Danny turned the truck back into the street and we started combing the back streets, again pausing to inspect every parked truck we saw. About fifteen minutes later we saw a truck at the side of the street, and we slowed once more.

"Jake!" Caroline said excitedly. "I think—yes, that's the truck!"

Danny braked hastily, and we all scrambled out. Caroline ran up and tapped on the window of the cab. "Stanley, are you all right?" she asked.

A young man with a round face was dozing in the front seat. He woke up and rolled down the window.

"Oh, hi, Caroline. Did you come to fix the truck?" he asked, his tone trusting. "Mr. Powers told me to watch it, and I did."

"You did a good job, Stanley," Caroline told him gently. "No, we're not going to fix the truck just yet. Right now we need to take all these boxes and move them into the back of our truck. Would you like to help us?"

"Uh-huh," he said. "Your mom says I'm a big help, Caroline."

"I know you are, Stanley," Caroline agreed. "Let's get to work, okay? We don't have much time."

Stanley produced a key and we unlocked the back of the big truck. The four of us lifted boxes full of presents and set them carefully into the back of Danny's pickup. We soon had all the boxes loaded and secured.

"Now we've got to get to the center before they give up and go home," I suggested.

Caroline pulled me aside. "We can't leave Stanley sitting in a cold truck," she said. "He needs to come with us."

I looked at the truck cab. Three was already too tight; four wouldn't make it. "Want me to stay here? It's Danny's truck, and you know where the center is."

She shook her head. "No way. You're the one who got this going. If you wouldn't mind me sitting in your lap"—her cheeks turned pink—"we can manage."

Like I would mind. "Okay," I said, and we all piled into the truck. Caroline put one arm lightly around me, and I held her so she wouldn't hit the windshield when the truck hit a bump. She didn't weigh as much as I expected, and the soft fabric of her dress rustled as she shifted to look out the window. I loved having her close to me; I wanted the ride to last all night. But we got to the center within ten minutes.

Caroline climbed out first and ran in to let everyone know that the gifts had arrived. The rest of us unloaded the boxes and took them all in through the back door. A man in a Santa suit was there, wiping his brow.

"You found them!" he said. "Wonderful! I ran out of jokes and candy canes a long time ago."

Caroline's mother came into the back room and helped us put the boxes into Santa's bags. "Jake, Caroline told me this was your idea. How can I thank you? I'm sorry if we've ruined your evening."

She didn't know that riding through the darkness with Caroline so close was worth leaving any dance. "This was more important," I said, nodding toward the gifts.

"Do you want to get back to the dance right away?" she asked.

Glancing at my watch, I figured that the crowning had already taken place; another few minutes here would make little difference. "Is it okay if I watch them give out the presents to the kids?"

She smiled at me. "Of course. Do you want to be an elf and help hand them out?"

I laughed. "Okay." I took off my coat and gloves, and Caroline's mom found us all red Santa hats. The hat didn't *quite* go with my tux; I thought I made a pretty silly-looking elf. But Caroline looked just right; the shimmering red dress made her cheeks rosy and her eyes sparkle.

We each picked up a bag of gifts. When Santa went out to the front room, ho-ho-hoing and taking his seat, we followed. Squeals of excitement rose when the children saw the gifts pour out of the bags.

I stood by the side and handed gifts to Santa, who would call out the name on the box. Each kid came up when called. One little girl with a headful of dark braids came up shyly and accepted a large box, her eyes wide with excitement. The next child was a small freckled boy with red hair. I listened carefully when Santa called the boys' names. Where was Kevin?

At last Santa called "Kevin." A small boy with shaggy brown hair and big brown eyes walked up slowly. He looked at the big, red-suited man in the chair as if unsure what would happen if he got too close.

The shirt Kevin wore was short at the cuffs and ragged along the collar, but it was clean. His hair had been carefully combed, and he had cookie crumbs on his chin.

Santa smiled at him and offered him the stack of boxes I had wrapped so carefully at home. I hoped he would like the truck I had picked out, and the clothes too. Kevin's eyes were wide as he looked at the boxes.

"Are they all for me?" he asked, so low that I could hardly catch the words. "Just me?"

"Just you," Santa told him, smiling beneath his fake beard.

Kevin took the boxes and went back to the side of the room to join a girl who looked like she could have been his little sister. She had already opened a box of her own. A woman—she might have been their mother—beamed at them. I watched Kevin, trying not to be obvious.

When he opened the first box and took out the sweater, he touched it gently, then yanked it out and pulled it over his head. For a moment he was stuck, turtlelike, arms waving. Then his head popped through the opening. Laughing, he arranged the sweater, then looked down at himself proudly.

I felt a lump in my throat and swallowed hard. He looked so happy. He went through the rest of the clothes rapidly, then found the toy truck and was soon absorbed in pushing it around the floor, crawling on his hands and knees and softly saying, "Varoom," as he steered it.

I turned and saw Caroline watching me. "You're a good guy, Jake," she said. "You made all this possible, you know. I'm—my mom and her volunteers—they're really grateful. And the kids and their families—they won't know, of course, but—"

"It doesn't matter," I said, feeling embarrassed. "I don't need any thanks. Seeing that"—I gestured toward the noisy crowd of children, the open parcels, the small girl waving her arms in a new coat, the toddler with a new teddy bear, Kevin still pushing his truck happily across the floor—"that's more than enough."

And I made Caroline smile again, I thought. *For all the right reasons.* That was the icing on the cake. How long would I have to wait before I could tell her how I felt? I ached to step a little closer, to put my arms around her—I thought of the too brief ride in the truck and sighed. Would I ever get to kiss those smooth lips, touch her cheek, hold her in my arms?

Caroline looked at me, then away. "I guess we should get back. The dance has another hour or so to go."

She wanted to finish the night with her date. My mood plummeted. "Sure," I said gloomily. "Let's get Danny."

Before we left, Mrs. Willis thanked me again and "Santa" shook my hand heartily. "You came to the rescue just like that red-nosed reindeer," he told me, chuckling.

Stanley stayed with Mrs. Willis so she could see him home safely. Now there was no excuse for Caroline to sit on my lap. I was still trying to figure out how to let her know how I felt about her. When I put my arm lightly around her shoulders, she didn't seem to mind. I didn't want to waste my last few minutes with her, especially not if I had to hand her over to Wade when we reached the hotel.

"What happened to you?" Sid shouted to me as I walked into the ballroom. "Shelley and I went to get our pictures taken, and when I came back, I heard you were off chasing Santa Claus."

I laughed. "Something like that," I told him. I stared out at the dance floor, trying to find Miranda. I soon found her in the middle of the dance floor, swaying in Chad's arms. A crown sat firmly on her blond head. *Chad better look out*, I thought, *if he doesn't want to get bitten by—*

"The blond barracuda," Sid murmured as if he could read my mind. He pointed out toward the floor with an exaggerated gesture. "Just look at that, wouldya? How could that sweet girl do something like this to you?" he asked, half jokingly.

"Miranda can do whatever she wants from now on," I said, shaking my head. "I just don't care anymore."

"Are you cured, Jake?" Sid asked.

"Yeah, I'm cured," I replied. I stared out at the floor a while longer, feeling a twinge in my chest. Miranda was dancing with Chad, Sid had Shelley, Caroline was off somewhere with Wade . . . what a night. I turned to Sid. "Hey, when you're ready to leave, would you mind—would you and Shelley mind giving me a lift back to Miranda's house so I can pick up my car?"

Sid grinned and looked at Shelley, who nodded and smiled. "Sure, we'll drop you off before we go out for a late night snack."

"Unless you want to come along?" Shelley added.

"No, thanks," I told her. "I don't want to horn in on the end of your big night."

The band struck up a new song, and Shelley motioned to Sid. He stood up and held out his hand, and they walked out to the dance floor.

I couldn't let myself sit and watch everyone else having a good time. I stood up again and wandered out into the hall. At the far end a tall window overlooked the street. I walked over to see if it was snowing again. The night sky was clear, and only a few cars zoomed up and down the avenue.

I was really and truly alone. Some way to end the big holiday dance.

I saw the reflection in the window glass before I heard the muffled footsteps on the carpet. I knew at once who it was, and I turned quickly.

"Caroline!"

She was alone. Where was Wade?

"You okay?" she asked. "I saw Miranda inside dancing with Chad. Kara's in the ladies' room, fuming and plotting revenge." She smiled. "I wondered how you were."

"I'm fine, I guess," I told her. "Miranda got her crown. That's what she really wanted from the evening. She and I are history."

"And you don't mind?" Caroline asked.

"I'm relieved," I told her honestly. "What about you and Wade? Everything okay?"

"Fine," she echoed my answer.

"Oh," I murmured. The disappointment in my tone must have been pretty obvious because Caroline laughed.

"Since you're so good at coming to the rescue, Jake, I thought you might do me a favor," she added.

"Sure," I replied, mystified.

"Maybe you could give me a ride home?" She tried to keep her expression serious, but her lower lip wobbled a little, and I saw the laughter in her eyes.

"B-B-But what about Wade?" I sputtered, feeling hope bubble inside me once again.

"Wade and I are just friends," she explained to me solemnly while her hazel eyes twinkled. "Guys and girls do that sometimes, you know; just go around as friends."

"So I've heard," I told her, feeling a smile creep across my face.

She took a step closer. I wrapped my arms around her waist and pulled her toward me, feeling the smooth fabric of her dress and the warmth of her skin as she put her arms around my neck. She was as sweet as Christmas candy, as warm as a roaring fire on a cold night.

Finally I was kissing Caroline, and the buzzing in my head was louder than the music that drifted from the ballroom. The kiss seemed to last forever and yet not long enough.

When we finally pulled apart, we were both breathless. "Are we friends again?" I asked Caroline.

"Oh, no, Jake, we're not friends," she replied, touching my cheek lightly. "We're much more."

I felt warmth spread through me as I leaned in for another kiss. "Merry Christmas, Caroline."

"Merry Christmas, Jake," she whispered as her lips touched mine. "Merry Christmas."

LOVE STORIES
Holiday Love Quiz

The holiday season always brings lots of parties, family gatherings, and dances. Maybe you've found a guy to be your permanent date for every event. But are you two meant to be, or will it all be over on New Year's Day? Take Jenny and Jake's special quiz to find out. P.S. Be honest!

1. *Would you send his family a holiday card?*
   A. Yes. The prettiest, most expensive one you can find.
   B. No. You're not quite sure where they live.
   C. You'd like to, but you'd probably ask what he thinks first.

2. *You're wrapped in his arms, nestled in front of a warm fire. You're thinking:*
   A. I hope we'll be a couple like this for many winters to come.
   B. This is nice. He's so cuddly!
   C. Should I wear my red leggings or my plaid skirt tomorrow?

3. *The perfect gift for your guy is:*
   A. Something romantic or funny, like silk Mickey Mouse boxers.
   B. Something useful, like a tie to wear to his family get-togethers.
   C. Something to improve himself, like an oxford shirt to replace his dingy flannels.

4. *He invites you to a holiday dinner with his family. You say:*
   A. "You must be kidding. *A Very Brady Christmas* is on!"
   B. "That sounds nice. I'd love to."
   C. "I'll come an hour early to help your mom get ready—and I'll bring my famous banana nut bread too."

5. *Would you invite him to celebrate with your family?*
   A. Definitely! You'd love to include him in family pictures.
   B. Maybe. But only if your parents promise not to wear their matching reindeer costumes.
   C. No way. Family stuff is family stuff.

6. *Your boyfriend attempts to make potato latkes for Hanukkah but burns them beyond recognition. You:*

A. Eat as many as you can and tell him you loved them.

B. Tell him to stay away from any and all kitchens.

C. Smile and feed them to the dog.

7. *You're at a party and he notices you're standing under the mistletoe. When he tries to kiss you, you:*

A. Let him peck you on the cheek.

B. Respond enthusiastically.

C. Tell him, "Not in public!"

8. *You've gone caroling with friends every year and had a great time. Do you invite him along this year?*

A. Yes—but you wouldn't push it.

B. Absolutely. You wouldn't have any fun without him there.

C. No. He can't sing and he'd bring you all down.

9. He invites you to watch him play snow football with a bunch of friends. You:

A. Bring hot chocolate and cookies for halftime.

B. Bundle up and cheer for as long as you can, then fake a stomach cramp and go home.

C. Tell him you don't like football in the first place and knee-deep snow just makes it even more unappealing.

10. His Christmas gift to you is a horrendously ugly sweatshirt that you can't imagine putting on your body. You:

A. Wear it to work out at home and let him see you in it from time to time.

B. Take it back and exchange it for something you like.

C. Tell him to take it back. He obviously pays no attention to your style.

11. He can't wrap presents to save his life and asks for your help. You say:

A. "Let me handle it. I love making bows and writing gift tags."

B. "Do I look like an elf?"

C. "Okay. We can work on it together."

12. *He invites you over for a night of Kwanza. The customs are new to you and you feel a bit awkward. You:*
- A. Spend all your free time researching the holiday in the library.
- B. Show up but make an excuse to bow out early.
- C. Ask him to clue you in on what to expect.

13. *His friends are all coming over to watch* Ernest Saves Christmas *and he asks you to come. You've always thought it was a stupid movie. You:*
- A. Tell him you're a little too intelligent for that, but if he wants to melt his brain for the holidays, he should feel free.
- B. Tell him yes but force him to watch *Miracle on 34th Street*—the classic black-and-white version—afterward.
- C. Say you'd love to, then force yourself to laugh when he and his friends do.

14. *It's time for your last-minute shopping spree. Do you invite him along?*
- A. Yes. He'd probably help keep you sane.
- B. Absolutely not. He'd just get in the way.
- C. No way! You need to buy more presents for him!

15. *You and your guy get your picture taken at the mall with Santa Claus. The picture ends up:*
  A. In the back of your desk drawer.
  B. In a frame on your desk.
  C. In your memory album.

Scoring: Give yourself the corresponding number of points for each answer.

1. A—2, B—0, C—1
2. A—2, B—1, C—0
3. A—2, B—1, C—0
4. A—0, B—1, C—2
5. A—2, B—1, C—0
6. A—2, B—0, C—1
7. A—1, B—2, C—0
8. A—1, B—2, C—0
9. A—2, B—1, C—0
10. A—2, B—1, C—0
11. A—2, B—0, C—1
12. A—2, B—0, C—1
13. A—0, B—1, C—2
14. A—1, B—0, C—2
15. A—0, B—2, C—1

The Verdict:

If your score is from 0 to 10:

We can't even figure out why you're together *now*, never mind the future. You don't show much compassion for or even interest in the guy you're dating. You don't seem to pay attention to him or try to take part in the things he likes. Ask yourself if it's *him* you really like or if you just like having a guy on your arm.

If your score is from 11 to 20:

This relationship is obviously important to you. You care about his interests and try to include him in yours. You enjoy being together but know how not to overdo it. Just remember to keep from overcrowding him and you may very well be celebrating together again next year!

If your score is from 21 to 30:

Back off a little bit, girl! You obviously really like this guy because you're willing to give up anything for him. Stop doing this as soon as possible! It's bad for you *and* for the relationship. He'll like you better if you retain your own personality and don't hang on him so much. If you want to make it through New Year's, take our advice: Be your own person.

Happy holidays!
And be safe!

Love,

Jenny & Jake